"This Is About You And Me, Rosebud.

This is about me liking you and you liking me, slow dances to fast songs and not going down without a fight. You promised me you wouldn't go down without a fight, and I'm going to hold you to that. Have dinner with me tonight."

"I can't."

Which was a hell of a lot different from "I won't."

"Someplace quiet," Dan continued. "That's all I want. Just you and me."

"What makes you think it would be any different the next time?" Her voice shook as she blinked rapidly and pulled away from him. "Or the time after that? Or any time? We can't hide forever. I can't, anyway."

Anger flashed through him. "I do *not* hide, Rosebud—and you don't, either."

* * *

Dear Reader,

This story began when an image popped into my head of an Indian Princess riding bareback out of the past and into the hero's present. Before the hero could figure out who she was, she took a shot at him and rode away. This image was so powerful that it stayed with me for months while the characters waited for me to figure out who they were, why she'd put a bullet through the hero's hat and, most important, how they could ever fall in love.

I like to think of this book as my Polaroid® book—the story took a long time to develop, but it was worth the wait. The hero turned out to be Dan Armstrong, the Chief Operating Officer of an energy company looking to build a hydroelectric dam. The heroine was Rosebud Donnelly, the tribal lawyer for the Red Creek Lakota, whose reservation will be flooded by Dan's dam. I imagined that having your whole world sunk to the bottom of an artificial lake was a good reason for a woman to be fighting-mad, and Rosebud agreed.

The surprise to Rosebud was how much Dan, an oil tycoon, turned out to be a man of principle and honesty. On top of all that integrity, he is one good-looking cowboy who knows his way around a horse—and a woman. He'll use all that charm to get to the bottom of who killed his hat. The question Dan has to answer is, what else is he willing to lose?

A Man of His Word is my first Harlequin Desire book, and for that alone, it will always be one of my favorites. I hope you enjoy reading it as much as I enjoyed writing it! Be sure to stop by www.sarahmanderson.com and join me when I say, long live cowboys!

Sarah

SARAH M. ANDERSON

A MAN
OF HIS WORD

Recycling programs
for this product may
not exist in your area.

ISBN-13: 978-0-373-73143-5

A MAN OF HIS WORD

www.Harlequin.com

Printed in U.S.A.

SARAH M. ANDERSON

Award-winning author Sarah M. Anderson may live east of the Mississippi River, but her heart lies out west on the Great Plains. With a lifelong love of horses and two history teachers for parents, she had plenty of encouragement to learn everything she could about the tribes of the Great Plains.

When she started writing, it wasn't long before her characters found themselves out in South Dakota among the Lakota Sioux. She loves to put people from two different worlds into new situations and see how their backgrounds and cultures take them someplace they never thought they'd go.

When not helping out at school or walking her two rescue dogs, Sarah spends her days having conversations with imaginary cowboys and American Indians, all of which is surprisingly well-tolerated by her wonderful husband and son. Readers can find out more about Sarah's love of cowboys and Indians at www.sarahmanderson.com.

To Mom and Dad, two history teachers who planned
family vacations around national monuments and
Civil War battle sites instead of theme parks and beaches.

One

For today's ride, Dan Armstrong had brought along his custom-made six-shooter, but he couldn't believe he'd need it.

He didn't normally wear it, but his uncle had told him to take a gun if he went out alone. And since it had been years since the man had shown a whit of interest in Dan's well-being, he'd listened. Now he was glad he'd done so because his imagination was working overtime.

There was something about this forest that said Old West, South Dakota style. His sprawling estate outside of Fort Worth was a jewel, but north Texas didn't have stands of pines this pretty or the carved sandstone bluffs that ran along the Dakota River.

It was a damn shame the trees, the river and the land wouldn't be the same once his company got done with them. His uncle, Cecil Armstrong, who ran one half of Armstrong Holdings, wanted to clear-cut these hundreds of acres before building a dam on this river, about five hundred yards upstream. No sense in throwing away perfectly good logging rights, Cecil had said. Logically, Dan couldn't argue with that, but he'd hate to see this forest go.

He didn't doubt that this place looked the same today as it had hundreds of years ago, back when cowboys and Indians rode the range. If he closed his eyes, he could almost hear war whoops and the thunder of hooves.

He twisted in the saddle, squinting as he looked into the afternoon sun. He really did hear hoofbeats.

The sound stopped when he moved, and by the time he got his eyes shaded with the brim of his Stetson, all he could see was a dust cloud about a hundred yards back, down the well-worn deer path he'd come in on.

Instinctively, Dan dropped his hand to the butt of his pistol. Sure, the engraved nickel firearm was only good for six shots, but he'd wanted a piece that was specifically weighted to his grip.

His hand flexed around the gun and waited. The dust settled around a figure. The sunlight provided an almost sparkly air around her. He blinked. What he saw didn't change, so he shook his head. Still there.

A Native American princess sat astride a paint horse. Her hair hung loose behind her, blowing in a breeze that Dan couldn't feel. He couldn't feel much of anything but sheer shock. *What the hell?*

Her horse took a step closer. She wore nothing but an old-fashioned, unadorned buckskin dress that rode high up on lean thighs that clung to the sides of her paint horse with natural ease. It was clear this princess knew how to ride bareback. The length of her legs ended with simple moccasins. Her horse's face was coated in red. Was that war paint?

Could this be happening? She looked like she belonged to a different time, as pure and untouched as the land around her. He'd seen a few Lakota Indians in the three days since he'd arrived, but none of them looked like this.

None of them looked at him like she was looking at him.

One of her hands held the reins of her horse, the other was relaxed by her leg. She tilted her head, sending all that black hair off to one side. She was stunning. A princess of the high plains.

Dan's heartbeat picked up and he slid his hand away from his revolver. She was not what he expected. Cecil had warned him that the local Lakota Indians were a bunch of lazy drunks—but not this woman. The proud way she held her body as her clear eyes swept over him made it obvious that neither of those adjectives applied to her. He'd never seen a woman as stop-what-he's-doing-and-stare beautiful as she was. She leaned forward, and he caught the shape of her buckskin-clad chest. His pulse wasn't the only thing that picked up. What the hell was wrong with him?

The princess flashed him a smile, which didn't help. He had trouble reading her expression at this distance, but there was no mistaking the wide grin or the brightness of her teeth. Then, as quickly as she'd smiled, she was a blur of motion. Her horse shot forward in the same second her hand shot up. His hat went flying as an explosion rocked the valley.

His horse jumped and spun, and Dan lost track of the woman. His first instinct was to rein in Smokey; his second was to duck for cover. That explosion had sounded a hell of a lot like a gunshot.

By the time he got his stallion turned back around, she was gone. Dan didn't think, he just acted. He touched his spurs to the horse's side and took off for the deer trail. Fueled by adrenaline, he plunged into the shadowy woods. Beautiful or no, no one took a shot at him. No one.

He could hear the sound of a large body crashing through the underbrush, over to his left. Whoever she was, she was abandoning the deer path. Dan blinked hard, forcing his eyes to adjust to the dim light. He thought he caught a flash of white ahead.

The harder he rode, the madder he got. In the oil business, he'd dealt with plenty of shady characters—men with agendas or histories—but no one had ever taken an unprovoked shot at him. Hell, no one had ever taken a shot at him, period. He didn't have enemies because he didn't make them. That "man-against-the-world" crap might have been the way of things back in the old days, but Dan was no gunslinger. He was a businessman—a successful one. His word was his bond, and his lawyer rode herd when a deal went south.

He caught the flash of white again and froze.

A white-tailed deer was high-tailing it away from him.

Cursing, Dan pulled Smokey to a stop and tried to figure out what the hell had happened. Maybe it hadn't been real. People imagined sounds, right? But then he remembered his hat. It had come off in the confusion. No matter what had actually happened, he wasn't going to leave his hat. He loved that hat—it fit his head perfectly. Slowly, Dan worked his way back down to the tall grass until he saw the brown brim of his Stetson. He got down to fetch it.

His gut clenched in a terrifying rage. A hole pierced the front peak of the hat, less than an inch from where it had rested on his head.

She'd shot at him. That beautiful woman—bare legs, bareback—had shot at him.

Somebody owed him an explanation.

Dan was still plenty steamed by the time he got back to the ranch house. For some crack-brained reason, his uncle had decided to set up the hydro division of Armstrong Holdings in one of those grand old mansions some cattle baron had built back in the 1880s. As far as mansions went, it was a beautiful piece of work—three floors of hand-carved banisters and stained-glass windows on sixty acres—but corporate headquarters it wasn't. Why Cecil was camped out on the edge of the middle of nowhere, halfway between the state capital in Pierre and the Iowa border, instead of at the small staffed office he had in Sioux Falls was beyond him. It was almost like the old man was trying to hide.

As chief operating officer of Armstrong Holdings, the family business that Dan's father had started with his brother Cecil forty years ago, Dan owned half of this house. Technically, he owned half of the water rights on the Dakota River over which the Red Creek branch of the Lakota Indian tribe was suing Cecil. He owned half of that pretty little valley where his hat had met an untimely death. Technically, he was an equal partner in this whole damn enterprise, and had been since he'd assumed control of the petroleum division in Texas from his mother when he turned twenty-one.

He'd be damned if he let Cecil destroy the company he'd worked so hard to expand.

Cecil had never been one for technicalities, an opinion made abundantly clear last week when he'd ordered Dan to drop everything in Texas and come to South Dakota. Cecil had a problem with the dam he'd spent nearly five years trying to build and had threatened that Armstrong Holdings would lose billions of dollars and just about every government contract they had if Dan didn't get his ass on a plane within a week.

Dan hated to let anyone think he was at the old man's beck and call—least of all, the old man himself—but this problem with the dam gave Dan the perfect opportunity to come up here and figure out what those little—and not so little—blips in the company's financial reports were all about. He didn't know what exactly he was looking for, but he knew he wouldn't find it in Texas. He was going to have to suffer his uncle until he could force Cecil out of the role of chief executive officer.

Now that he thought about it, Dan remembered that it was Cecil who had warned him about the local Indians—that he was having trouble with negotiations with some of them. Dan just hadn't realized that the problem would require body armor and a helmet.

The gabled roof of the ranch house looked even more ominous as the late-afternoon sun cast deep shadows over the front yard. The cast-iron fence looked less like it wanted to keep Cecil's old coon dog in and more like it wanted to keep armed assailants out. Dan stormed through the front door, making the housekeeper jump.

"Is everything all right, Señor Armstrong?" Maria's thick Mexican accent was the closest thing to Texas in this whole house.

Dan slowed. From what he could tell, Cecil treated this poor woman like dirt, which made Dan go out of his way to be polite. Being friendly with the staff had always helped him in the past—especially when he needed information. Mom always said Dan could catch more flies with honey when he wanted to, and right now, he had a bunch of flies bothering him. "Maria," he said, his voice slipping down just a notch as he whipped off his hat. Her cheeks colored. "Do you all have trouble around here?"

The color deepened as she dropped her eyes to the ground. Dan guessed that maybe thirty years ago, Maria had been quite a looker. He didn't mean to make her blush, but sweet-talking a woman was second nature for him. "Trouble, *señor?*"

"Native American trouble?" Maria blinked in confusion, so Dan tried again. "Indian trouble?" Even saying the phrase felt wrong, like it was the 1880s and he was stuck in the middle of a range war. He cleared his throat. If it weren't for the bullet hole in his hat, he'd be certain he'd lost his mind. He held his hat out to her.

Maria went very still as she looked at the hole, and then at his head. *"Dios mi!* No, *señor,* we do not have that kind of trouble."

Damn. Dan was good at reading people, women in particular. Maria was telling the truth.

"You'll let me know if you hear of any, won't you?" He shot her his *please* smile.

Her head bobbed as she began to back toward the kitchen. *"Sí, señor."*

Satisfied, he continued on to his uncle's office. It had probably once been the formal dining room, capable of seating twenty, but no more. Now it was crammed full of everything a man needed to run a major energy corporation. In Texas, Cecil had been a ruthless businessman, squeezing out small-time operations and buying land for astonishing prices. By the time the SUV craze rolled around, he held a near monopoly on Texas oil.

Cecil was whip-smart. By the time the writing was on the fossil fuel wall, he'd invested deeply in hydroelectric dams. That's what had brought him to South Dakota. The water rights were cheap up here, and the potential was huge. Armstrong Hydro was quickly becoming not just the major player in the field, but the only player.

Dan didn't like the man, never had. Not one bit. But family was family, and Cecil and Dan were tied by blood and by business. Dan couldn't get rid of the old man without hard evidence of malfeasance that he could present to the Board of Directors. Maybe on this trip, he'd find just what he needed to finally cut their connection. Without breaking stride, he burst into the room.

"Well?" Cecil demanded without bothering to look up from the report he was studying. The old man still had the same pompadour and trimmed mustache he'd worn since the 1950s. The only thing that had changed in five years were the jowls Cecil was now sporting. Those jowls, combined with the careful grooming, made Cecil look like the poster boy for the banality of evil. Emphasis on the *evil*. Those pictures of Cecil and his brother Lewis, Dan's father, with their first oil derrick were the only proof Dan had ever seen that his uncle smiled. He'd certainly never smiled at Dan—not once.

Dan gritted his teeth and threw his hat on the desk. The hole landed directly in front of Cecil's face. "Someone took a shot at me."

Cecil appeared to study the wounded hat for a moment. "Did you get them?" He didn't sound concerned or surprised.

"No. I lost her."

A sneer wrestled one corner of Cecil's mouth up. "You let a *girl* get off an unanswered shot?"

He didn't have to defend himself here. Cecil had told him to pack his revolver. "Thanks for the warnin'."

"Are you sure it was a girl?" The sneer didn't falter.

Dan thought back to the lean, bare thighs, the long hair and that smile. Girl, no. Woman? Hell, yes. "Positive."

"No one's seen...*her* before." Cecil hadn't known a woman was out there? He seemed to be struggling to digest the information. "If it's the same troublemaker, she's sabotaged the engineer's work site on more than one occasion."

He had heard about the trouble with the work site, but only third-hand from an engineer Cecil had sent packing. Cecil apparently didn't believe an ecoterrorist attack on an Armstrong project was worth reporting to the board—yet another thing he was hiding. How many other things were there?

Dan had dealt with ecoterrorists before. The Earth Liberation Front—ELF—had burned more than a few of his derricks before Dan had managed to negotiate a truce of sorts. But even ELF had never gone to all the trouble of disguises in broad daylight. They'd been strictly an under-cover-of-night group, more bent on the destruction of property than of people. He could handle ecoterrorists. What he couldn't handle were armed—and beautiful—Native American princesses.

Without missing a beat, Cecil threw Dan's hat back at him and picked up a sheaf of paper from the top of a neat pile. "I have a new assignment for you."

Dan's teeth ground together. An *assignment*. Cecil always tried to treat Dan like he was some two-bit underling instead of an equal partner. Like that little bit of self-delusion gave the old man sole control of the company. "Anyone going to be firing on me this time?"

Cecil let the comment slide. "I'm sending you to meet with the Indians. You're better at—" his hands waved like he could grab hold of a word out of thin air "—talking."

There's an understatement, Dan thought with a concealed snort. Cecil didn't talk. Cecil ordered. "Why them?"

"It's a bunch of bull. They think they're going to get an injunction against the dam construction over water rights— rights I already own."

"That *we* already own. Don't you have lawyers? Why the hell do you need me for this?"

"The tribal lawyer is a bearcat. Rosebud Donnelly. She's eaten three of my lawyers for lunch." Cecil spat the words out with true disgust.

Rosebud? Like the sled from that old movie Mom loved? Couldn't be. Whoever she was, Dan felt a small thread of admiration for her. Anyone who could successfully stonewall his uncle was a person to be taken seriously. "And?"

Cecil looked him over with mercenary eyes. "You are an attractive man, son. Good with women. Hell, you treat that maid like she's some damn queen."

Dan's jaw stiffened. *Son.* He hated it when Cecil called him that. Dan was many things to Cecil, but a son he wasn't.

"You handled those ELF nuts in Texas. This is no different. She's just a woman."

Dan managed to clear his throat. "You want me to do what—sweep her off her feet so she forgets about suing us?" It was Cecil's turn to stiffen. *That's right,* Dan thought. *Us. This is my company, too.*

"All I'm suggesting is you distract her. And if you happen to get access to some of her files..." He let the words trail off, but the meaning was clear. He thought he could use Dan as nothing more than a male bimbo.

Dan snatched the papers out of Cecil's hand. The sooner he got out of this room, the better life would be. Just breathing Cecil's air was toxic. "Where?"

"On the reservation. Tomorrow at ten." Cecil waved his hand in dismissal.

For the second time that day, Dan was so mad he couldn't see straight. Cecil had known someone was out there. If Dan didn't know any better, he might be tempted to think the old man was trying to get him killed.

He looked down at the papers, a Google map to the tribal headquarters and some names. On one hand, he detested letting his uncle think Dan would do his heavy-handed bidding. On the other hand, if Cecil was having "problems" with Indians, maybe they had something on him, something Dan could use. Besides, if a man was looking for a Native American princess packing a pistol, the reservation was the place to be.

He was going to start with one Rosebud Donnelly.

Two

Rosebud Donnelly looked over the rims of her glasses to see Judy, the receptionist, standing in the doorway with an unusual look of confusion on her face.

"He's here."

"Johnson came back for more?" Here, in the privacy of her office—even if it was just a modified broom closet—Rosebud allowed herself to smile at the thought of that twit Johnson breaking. A pitiful excuse for a lawyer, that one.

"No." Judy's eyes got wider.

"It's not *that man,* is it?" She couldn't imagine that Cecil Armstrong would actually show himself in public, in daylight. She'd never met him, but she imagined him to be some sort of vampire, except instead of sucking blood, he was hellbent on draining her reservation dry—and then flooding it.

"He said his name was Dan Armstrong. He said he was Cecil's nephew."

The satisfaction was intense. She was getting to *that man.* Cecil Armstrong had run out of high-priced lawyers who wouldn't know tribal law from a hole in the ground. He'd been reduced to family—as if Rosebud could be swayed by emotional pleas. "A regular mini-me, huh?"

"No," Judy said again, her voice dropping. "He's...something else entirely. Be careful with this one, Rosebud."

Judy's befuddlement was worrisome. "I'm always careful." Which was true. She took no chances—she couldn't afford to. "He can sit. Make sure he's got coffee—plenty of coffee," she added with a nod. She preferred her sworn enemies to be as uncomfortable as possible. "And let me know when Joe and Emily get here."

After Judy left to go perk another pot of coffee, Rosebud took the time to break out her pitiful makeup bag. Her good looks were just one of her weapons, but she considered them her first best line of defense when meeting a new adversary.

After three years of representing the tribe in their dealings with Armstrong Holdings, she'd honed her game plan to perfection. Johnson was just the latest victim. Rosebud had played the bubble-headed babe for three weeks—long enough for Johnson to be sure he had the upper hand and, more importantly, long enough for Rosebud to secure some rather incriminating pictures of the man meeting with a supplier of prescription painkillers. Although he'd made bail, Johnson had recused himself from the case rather than tangle with Rosebud again.

Men, she thought with a snort. Especially *white* men. They all thought the rules applied to everyone else. She plaited her hair and wound the braid into a bun that projected both an old-fashioned innocence and an austere severity. To hold the bun in place, she inserted two sticks that would have looked like chopsticks, except for the bright green beaded tassels hanging from the ends. The sticks were the only things of her mother's she'd kept.

Her lipstick set, Rosebud gathered up her files. She held

no hope that this Dan Armstrong would be different from the others—after all, that rat-bastard Cecil had sent him—but there was always a small chance that he'd let something slip that could be connected back to her brother Tanner.

Judy knocked on the door. Rosebud glanced at the clock. Almost half an hour had passed. Perfect. "They're here."

"How do I look?" Rosebud batted her eyes.

"Be careful," Judy repeated, sounding awed.

Oh, Rosebud couldn't wait to see this guy, not if he was throwing Judy for such a loop. She met Joe White Thunder and Emily Mankiller outside the conference room. "Did Judy tell you it's a new guy?" she said as she kissed her aunt on the cheek.

Joe's eyes sparkled, and in that second, Rosebud saw the man who'd occupied Alcatraz back in the day. Some days, she longed to have known old Joe back when he raised a lot of hell, but she appreciated who he was now—a tribal elder whose vote carried a lot of weight. "I knew that last one was no match for you."

Rosebud blushed under the compliment as Aunt Emily shook her head at Joe in disapproval. Aunt Emily had never been one for disobedience, civil or otherwise. "You're making a dent, dear, but don't get overconfident."

Whatever, Rosebud thought as she nodded in deferential agreement. Cecil Armstrong had thrown the best lawyers money could buy at her, and she was not only holding them off, she was officially irritating *that man.* "I know. You guys remember what to do?"

Joe playfully socked her in the arm. *"How, kemo sabe."* And then his face went blank and Rosebud stood in front of the stereotypical Stoic Indian. Joe wouldn't say a single thing today. His job was intimidating silence. Rosebud knew he wouldn't even look at Dan Armstrong. If there was one thing self-important lawyers hated, it was being ignored. It drove them to distraction, and a distracted lawyer was a defeated lawyer.

Aunt Emily sighed. Rosebud knew she hated these meetings, hated all the haggling and hated it when Joe acted like a fake Indian. But she hated the idea of Armstrong Holdings flooding the rez more. "We're ready."

Here we go, Rosebud thought to herself as she opened the door. Her blood started to pump with excitement. Another adversary was another battle, and Rosebud was confident she could win the battles. She honestly didn't know if she could win the war with Cecil Armstrong, but she could slow him down for years.

The first thing she noticed was that Dan Armstrong was standing. His back was to the door and he was looking out the conference room's sliver of a window. The prick of irritation was small. She preferred her victim to be sitting in the chair that was two inches shorter than the others, with the bum wheel that gave the chair an unexpected wobble with every movement.

What she noticed next erased the irritation. Dan Armstrong was tall without being huge, his shoulders easily filling out the heathered brown sport coat. The brown leather yokes on his shoulders made his back seem even broader. She could see the curl in his close-cropped hair, the light from the window making it glow a golden-brown.

She caught her breath. Johnson he wasn't—in fact, she couldn't remember the last time she'd seen a real man in this building, a man who looked like he belonged out on the open range instead of in a dark little office. Hell, she couldn't remember the last time she'd seen a real man *outside* of this office.

And then he turned around.

Him. The breath she'd caught was crushed out of her chest. Suddenly she felt vulnerable, the kind of vulnerable that comes from making a mistake and then thinking she'd gotten away with it, only to be caught red-handed.

She was screwed.

He must have noticed her confusion, because he smiled the kind of smile a man wore when he knew exactly what effect he had on a woman. The implied arrogance—and not recognition—was enough to snap Rosebud out of her momentary terror. She might know who *he* was, but he didn't seem to recognize *her*. And if there were no witnesses, who was to say that a crime had occurred?

"Mr.…Armstrong, is it?" she began, striding into the room like she couldn't be bothered to remember his name. That's right, she thought as she drew herself up to her full height in three-inch heels, there wasn't a single thing wrong with any of this. Except he had a good four inches on her. "I'm Rosebud Donnelly, the lawyer for the Red Creek Lakota Indian reservation."

"A pleasure, ma'am." Oh, he had a faint drawl, a way of stretching out his vowels that sounded like warm sunshine. *Ma'am* had never sounded as good as it did coming out of his mouth. Armstrong lifted a hand as if to tip his hat, but then appeared to realize that he wasn't wearing one. Instead, he swung his hand down and offered it out to her. Rosebud wondered if he'd gone back for the hat she'd seen fly off his head, or if it was still out there. She'd have to check tonight. No hat, no crime.

Rosebud thanked God she'd done this enough to go on autopilot, because her head was swimming. Not one of the last three lawyers had even sniffed at a polite introduction. She let the seconds stretch as his hand hung in the air. Normally, she let her hand loosely clasp the other person's—all the better to create an impression of weakness—but not this time. This time, she felt an intense need to be in control of this situation. She returned his grip, noting that his hand was warm, but not sweaty. He wasn't nervous at all. She was going to have to do better, so she gave him her best bone-crushing shake.

He tilted his head to one side as if he was questioning her. Eyes the color of the sky right before a twister measured her with something that looked a hell of a lot like respect. God only knew what his uncle had told him about her—it probably started with *ball-buster* and ended with *bitch.* As the heat from his hand did a slow crawl up her arm, she had the sudden urge to tell him that she really wasn't like that.

Which was ridiculous—the whole point of this little introduction was to demonstrate that she was *exactly* like that. No wonder Judy had warned her about this one.

She stepped away from him, pulling her hand with her. He tried to keep his grip for just a second, then the firm pressure was gone. She shivered, but forced herself to forge ahead. "This is Joseph White Thunder, a tribal elder, and Councilwoman Emily Mankiller." Yes. Formal introductions were the next step. She needed to get back on track here.

Emily must have sensed Rosebud's hesitation, because she stepped into the gap. "Mr. Armstrong," she began as she and Joe took their seats without shaking hands, "are you familiar with the Treaty of 1877 between the United States government and the Lakota, Dakota and Nakota Sioux tribes of South Dakota?"

"Ma'am," Armstrong replied with a polite half bow as he sat down. Rosebud smiled internally as the whole thing tilted off-kilter and he clawed at the table to keep his balance. Still, he managed to sound nonplussed as he said, "I can't say that I am."

Thank God for that. Aunt Emily was one of the few women on this reservation with a master's degree in American history, and her role in this little meeting was to wear the adversary down with a complete recounting of the wrongs the Lakota Indians had suffered back in the day at the hands of the American government, and now, thanks to corporations such as Armstrong Holdings. Rosebud had about forty minutes to get her head together.

Aunt Emily droned on while Joe stared at a spot on the wall just over Armstrong's head. Rosebud unpacked her files and began reviewing her notes from the last go-round with Johnson. There wasn't much new to go on. Unlike with Johnson, usable dirt on Cecil Armstrong was just plain hard to dig up. He was courting both political parties, visited a respectable divorced woman twice a month in Sioux Falls and had no personal secretary. As far as she could tell, he hadn't ever set foot in the Armstrong Hydro office in Sioux Falls, and what few staffers worked there didn't seem to know anything. That was all she had after three years. It was frustrating.

She snuck a glance at Armstrong. Not only was he paying attention to Aunt Emily, he was taking notes. What the hell? Rosebud thought when Armstrong interrupted the lecture to ask for the specific dates of the last treaty signed. He must not be a lawyer, she decided. Lawyers didn't give a hoot for history lectures. Why would *that man* send someone who wasn't a lawyer?

Aunt Emily began to wind down when she got to the reason they were all here today. Rosebud waited as Armstrong finished his notes before she began. "*Mister* Armstrong," she began, going right past condescending and straight on over to contemptuous, "are you aware that Armstrong Holdings is preparing to dam the Dakota River?"

"Yes, ma'am," he replied, trying to lean back in the chair without tipping. "Down in a valley about two miles from here, as the crow flies. Armstrong Holdings owns the water rights and has secured the government permits to begin construction this fall."

Oh, she knew where the valley was. "And are you also

aware that the reservoir created by that dam will flood thirty-six hundred acres of the Red Creek reservation?"

Armstrong regarded her with open curiosity. "I understood the reservoir will cover several hundred square miles. I was told that land was mostly unoccupied."

Her eyes narrowed. What the hell was *that man* doing, sending an unarmed nephew into battle? He might as well have sent an errand boy instead of this…male. There was just no way around it. Everything about Dan Armstrong said *male,* from the good—no, great—chin to the way he sat in that chair, legs spread wide like he was just itching to get back on his horse.

God, he'd looked so good on that horse. Looking had been her first mistake. Instead of just firing over his head from the shadows like she'd planned, she'd wanted to get a better view of the behind that had been sitting in that saddle, a better look at the forearms laid bare for the sun. She'd come out of the shadows, and he'd spotted her. She'd nearly shot his head off, all because he was a man who looked good in a saddle.

She had to remind herself that, at this exact moment in time, she was not a woman, no matter how much she might like to be one. Right now, she was a lawyer, damn it. Men and women didn't count in a courtroom, and she couldn't afford for them to count in this conference room. The only thing that mattered was the law. "Then this is just a waste of our time, isn't it?" She stood and began to shove paper back into the files. Aunt Emily and Joe scrambled to their feet.

"Ms. Donnelly, please." Armstrong rose to his feet, too, which didn't make Rosebud any happier, because nothing good could come from looking up into those green-gray eyes. The only other option was to look at his jaw, which was strong and square and freshly shaved. "Educate me."

Educate him? After that history lesson, he was coming back for more? Suddenly, Rosebud realized just how great a danger Dan Armstrong was. She knew how to fight against faceless corporate stool pigeons. She had no idea what to do with a real man who apparently had a grasp on compassion—and already had her at a disadvantage. The feeling of helplessness left her with only one other emotion to grab at—anger.

"Fine." She unpacked all the files again at a rate that struck even her as irritated. "Cecil Armstrong has been a blight upon this land since he came here five years ago. He's strong-armed local ranchers—many with whom we had unspoken agreements—out of their water rights and lands. He's filed frivolous lawsuits against the tribe and attempted to use eminent domain as legal justification for taking our land." Eminent domain was the biggest threat to her whole legal standing, the one she knew she'd lose. Who the hell cared about a few hundred Indians when they could get their electricity for pennies-on-the-kilowatt cheaper? No one, that's who. No one but the tribe.

Armstrong sat down and began scribbling furiously. If this was an act, it was a damn good one, she decided. This must be why *that man* had sent him. The new, caring face of Armstrong Holdings. When he paused, she continued.

"He has engaged in a campaign of intimidation against members of the tribe." And wouldn't it be lovely if she had some proof of that? But who else would be responsible for Aunt Emily's shot-out windows or Joe's missing spark plugs and punctured tires? Who else would have left another skinned raccoon spread-eagled on her front porch three days ago? No one, that's who. No one else hated her with the passion of Cecil Armstrong.

"That's a serious charge," Dan said without looking up. His voice held steady, with no trace of knee-jerk denial.

"Men have died." Too late, she realized her voice was cracking. Aunt Emily reached out and rested a calming hand on Rosebud's arm. Dang it, she was losing her cool in a meeting. She *never* lost her cool.

Armstrong raised his eyes to meet hers. "Do you have proof?" It didn't come out sneering. It was just a simple question.

With a complicated answer. "The FBI determined that both cases were suicides. The tribal police didn't agree. Nothing ever came of it." Because money talks. The tribe had no money. Cecil Armstrong, it seemed, had it all. Broken, drunk Indians shot their heads off all the time. What were another two? Who cared that Tanner had never had a drink before in his life? He was just another Indian—who'd realized the danger Armstrong Holdings posed to the tribe from the beginning. Who'd happened to be making a run at the tribal council. Who'd happened to be her brother. Just another Indian, that's all.

Armstrong looked at her, then at Aunt Emily's hand, then back to her. "I'm sorry for your loss." And the hell of it was, he really seemed to mean it. Rosebud felt the ground shifting under her feet. Suddenly, she wasn't sure where she stood. "As I said, those are serious charges. I'd like to review your documents before I do anything else."

Finally, something technical she could hold on to. "I'm sure you can understand that we can't let the originals leave this building." *That man* would have himself one hell of a bonfire, that much she knew.

"Of course," he agreed far too easily. "Can you have a copy made for me?"

Another unpleasant reality smacked Rosebud upside the head. Of course this Dan Armstrong was used to a world where copiers worked. That world had shiny new computers that connected to the internet, real office space and chairs that didn't try to eat a person alive.

That wasn't her world.

She held her head high. "Your predecessor in negotiating, Mr. Lon Johnson, had a copy of all my files." Or at least, that was what he *thought*.

"Actually, I looked into that last night." Armstrong's mouth bowed up into an appreciative smile. "It appears that all those files up and disappeared out of his car one day, about a week ago. In addition to his laptop, iPod and three candy bars."

Hmm. That sounded like Matt, who was trying to fashion himself as the ideological heir to Tanner but thus far had just succeeded in being a low-level criminal. She would have loved to have gotten her hands on Johnson's laptop, but there was no question that it had already been pawned off or sold outright. Dang it, she thought. Another missed opportunity. She tried to look surprised, but given how Dan's grin got bigger, she didn't think she'd made it. "That's unfortunate." Armstrong cleared his throat. Time to go to the lame-excuse file. "Our copier recently had an...incident, shall we say. We are awaiting the parts." Which was only a small lie. The copier had had an incident, all right. Two years ago.

Armstrong seemed to buy it. "I guess that leaves only one other option. I'd like your permission," he said, directing his statement to all three of them, "to come back and review the files myself and take notes. That way, they don't leave the building, and I still get what I need."

Rosebud deferred to Aunt Emily, who was weighing the offer. Finally, she nodded. "Of course, Mr. Armstrong, you understand that there'll be conditions."

"Of course," he agreed, leaning back in the chair. He seemed to be getting used to the wobble. He looked to Rosebud, and again she saw the arrogant smile. A man used to getting his way. "I imagine you won't want me to have unsupervised access to original documents."

The implication was clear. He had her cornered, and they both knew it. Nobody else on the rez grasped the full import of all the details Rosebud had meticulously collected over the last three years, not even Aunt Emily. Rosebud was the only one who could possibly make sure nothing original "walked off." She was going to have to sit in this small room for hours—days—on end with a handsome, charming man while he copied her life's work by hand. He was going to leverage all that compassionate charm against her under the auspices of a fact-finding mission.

Whoever the hell Dan Armstrong was, she had to give him credit. He was a worthy opponent.

Aunt Emily took up her cue again. She began to go on about how the tribe just wanted to be left in peace and get a little respect from the outside world. Rosebud tuned her out. Instead, she found herself studying Armstrong's hands. He had calluses that told her he'd earned them the hard way. As he leaned back, she saw an impressive buckle that didn't look store-bought. Actually, upon closer inspection, she didn't think that his shirt was store-bought, either. She glanced down at his boots. Top-of-the-line alligator. They probably cost more than she took home before taxes last year. He wasn't some office gopher, but a man who worked and made more than a nice living. Somehow, she knew he didn't send anyone out to do his bidding. If this Dan Armstrong needed something done, he either asked the right person or he went and did it himself.

If she wasn't careful, she was going to be caught staring. She wondered what he'd been doing in the valley, and immediately, the guilt began to build. God, what a mess. She'd assumed he was one of Cecil Armstrong's mercenary "security" guards. That had been her second mistake. She couldn't be sure it had been her last one.

Finally, as Aunt Emily began to wind up, she noticed that Armstrong was starting to fidget in his chair. All that coffee was finally getting to him. Normally, she'd take advantage of his discomfort to really rake him over the coals, but not today. She needed to get out of this room, far away from this unusual man, and figure out her next move.

On Dan's way out the door, Joe still didn't shake Armstrong's hand, but Aunt Emily did. Then Dan shook Rosebud's hand. "I look forward to working with you," he said as he put the slightest pressure on her fingers. The warmth was still there, but this time it moved up her arm with a greater urgency until she was afraid her face was going to flush.

Damn. Damn, damn, damn. She was afraid she was looking forward to it, too.

Three

Rosebud was sure she'd thrown the files in her office and locked the door, but that part was a little hazy. The next thing she was really conscious of was the soft breeze and the warm sun on her face as she stood in the parking lot, facing south. The breeze still had a touch of cold spring in it, which was just enough to let her mind clear a little.

The situation was far from out of control, she quickly decided. Dan Armstrong might be a different kind of danger to her, but he was still just a man, and a woman didn't make it through law school without figuring out how to handle a man. She just needed to remember who he represented, not what he looked like or how he addressed her with all that "respect" and "compassion."

"You okay, Rosie?" Joe's hand rested on her shoulder.

"Oh, fine." Not true, but she was a lawyer, after all. Never admit weakness, because weakness is defeat. She opened her eyes to see Aunt Emily standing before her, a serious look on her face. "What?"

Aunt Emily looked to Joe and then sighed. "That man…"

"I can handle him."

Aunt Emily regarded her for a painful second. Then she leaned forward and grasped the sticks holding Rosebud's braided bun into place. The whole thing unfurled like a sail. "He is different. He is a handsome man, dear. And you are a handsome woman."

Something about the way she said it hit Rosebud funny. "What are you saying?"

"Keep your friends close, but your enemies closer," Joe said, sounding surprisingly serious about it. The weight of his hand suddenly felt like a vise, pinning her in place.

"You want me to—what? Sleep with him?" When Aunt Emily didn't say anything, Rosebud tried to take a step back, but Joe held her in place. The breeze—colder now, so cold it chilled her to the bone—caught the straggling remains of her braid and unwound it for her. "You *want* me to sleep with him?" Shame ripped through her.

Of all the things asked of her—leaving home for so many years to get that damned law degree when she really wanted to study art; giving up any semblance of a normal life to eat, drink and breathe legal proceedings against Armstrong Holdings; having dead animals show up around her house; losing her brother—sleeping with the enemy was the worst. Even if the enemy was as attractive as Dan Armstrong. That was irrelevant. It didn't matter that she'd given her life to the tribe. Now it wanted her body, too.

"No, no," Joe finally protested, too late. "But a beautiful woman can muddle a man's thinking."

"This may be the chance we've been waiting for, dear," Emily added. Rosebud could hear how little her aunt really believed it, but she kept going. "He could let something… useful slip about his uncle. He might know something about Tanner."

The blow was low. For a second, Rosebud wanted to smack the woman for pouring salt in her wound, but it was a short second. Of course, they were right. Dan Armstrong was an opportunity to do a little domestic spying, that was all. And if she could link Tanner's death to an Armstrong—any Armstrong—she'd be able to sleep at night. Hell, she might even find a new way to stop that dam.

Aunt Emily gave her an artificial smile. "It's what Tanner would do." She pulled Rosebud's glasses off her face and gently tucked them into the pocket of her one-and-only suit jacket. "Do it for Tanner."

Tears that she normally kept out of sight until the middle of the night, when no one would know she cried them, threatened to spill. She squeezed her eyes shut to keep them in. "All right," she managed to get out.

Aunt Emily kissed her cheek in painful blessing. "Find out what you can. Give away nothing."

"Do your best," Joe added, finally removing his clamping hand from her shoulder.

Her best. She'd been doing her best, fending off that dam for three years, but it hadn't been good enough. She wondered if anything ever would be.

She heard both car doors shut, heard both of them drive away, but still she couldn't open her eyes. The breeze tickled her hair, and the sun tried to reassure her it would, in fact, be all right, but she couldn't move. When Tanner had died, she'd sworn to do anything to find out who put that gun in his hand and pulled the trigger. She'd never thought it would come to seducing Cecil Armstrong's nephew.

"Ms. Donnelly?"

Oh, hell.

"Mr. Armstrong," she said without turning around. How on God's green earth was she supposed to muddle his thinking when her own mind was exactly as clear as the Dakota

River during the spring floods? "Thank you for coming today."

He stood next to her. She didn't know how she felt it, but one moment, she was alone, and the next, his solid warmth was close enough that she thought he was touching her arm. Moving slowly, she turned to meet his gaze.

As she did, the breeze surged like a trickster, throwing her hair around. The look in his eyes went from curious regard to recognition—the wrong kind of recognition. His nostrils flared as his jaw clenched. She was no longer facing a compassionate man. Any fool could see that Dan Armstrong was fighting mad.

"Tell me, Ms. Donnelly," he said through gritted teeth. "Do you ride?"

He knew—or thought he knew. In a heartbeat, she realized she needed to play innocent. "Of course. Everyone out here does. Do you?"

She couldn't even see those lovely greenish eyes. They were narrowed into slits. He wasn't buying it. "Sure do. What kind of horse do you ride?"

"Scout is a paint." She wanted to cower before that hard look, but she refused to break that easily. With everything she had, she met his stare. "Yours?"

"Palomino." He stepped around her so quickly that she couldn't help but flinch. "In fact, I was riding him near the dam site in a pretty little valley the other day."

"Is that so?" That was the best she could do as he threw open the door of an enormous, shiny black truck and yanked out a brown cowboy hat.

With a bullet hole through it.

She'd gotten a lot closer than she meant to. She hadn't actually been trying to hit him. She'd been trying to go right over his head, just close enough that he could hear the bullet. But she'd missed. She'd come within an inch of killing a man.

For the first time in her life, she felt really and truly faint. The only thing that kept her on her feet was the knowledge that fainting was a confession of the body. No weakness. No confession.

No matter if she was guilty of attempted murder.

Armstrong was watching her with cold interest. "Someone took a shot at me in that valley."

She managed to swallow, hoping that her reaction would be interpreted as mere shock and not guilt. "That's awful!" Her voice sounded decidedly strangled, even to her own ears. "Did you see who did it?"

He took a step toward her, until he was close enough that she could see how much his pupils had dilated. The almost-green was gone, replaced by a black so inky that he looked more like a *sica,* a spirit, than a man. "It was a woman." His voice was low and quiet, which gave him an air of danger. "A beautiful Native American woman with long, black hair." With his free hand, he reached out and grabbed a hank of her hair, twisting it around his hand until she had no way to escape. He pulled her face up to his. "Wearing buckskins and moccasins. Riding a paint."

Beautiful. She swallowed again. He smelled vaguely of coffee and horse, with a hint of something more exotic— sandalwood, maybe. He smelled *good.* And he was less than a minute from committing assault.

"Buckskins, Mr. Armstrong?" She paused long enough to muster up a look of slight disbelief. "Most of us prefer T-shirts and jeans these days." His mouth opened to protest, but she cut him off. "I can ask a few questions, Mr. Armstrong." Oh, thank God her lawyer voice had returned. She pressed on. "While we do not approve of your uncle's actions, we certainly wouldn't resort to attempted murder."

"A few questions?" His lips—nice, full lips, with just a

hint of pink—twisted into a full sneer as he leaned in even closer. "I want answers."

Friends close, enemies closer. She swallowed, and saw his eyes dart down to her mouth. This was playing with fire, but what else was there? "Are you going to kiss me?" Her lawyer voice was gone again, and instead she sounded like a femme fatale from a '40s film. Where that came from, she didn't know. She could only hope it was the right thing to say.

It was. His jaw flexed again, answering the question for her. Then his other hand moved, brushing a flyaway hair from her face and stroking her cheekbone with the barest hint of pressure. A quiver went through Rosebud, one she couldn't do a thing to stop. The corner of his mouth curled up, just enough to let her know that he'd felt that betraying quiver, too.

He wanted to kiss her, which should have made her feel successful—Aunt Emily would be proud. But his mouth had something else to say about the matter. "Are you fixing to take another shot at me?"

"I don't have any idea what you're talking about." She couldn't even manage to pull off indignant. The best she could do was a throaty whisper better suited to that kiss that still hung in the air between them.

His hand tightened around her hair. Oh, no, he wasn't about to let her off easy. "I thought lawyers were better liars."

Now she was back on more familiar footing. "That's funny. I always heard that liars were better lawyers."

Her stomach turned in anticipation. She'd been kissed, of course, but she'd never been hit. She had no idea which way this would go.

Kiss me. The thought popped into her head from a deep, primitive part of her brain that had nothing to do with Aunt Emily or self-defense. How long had it been since she'd been properly kissed? How long had it been since she'd been this close to a man who looked this good, a man who *smelled* this good? That primitive part of her brain did a quick tally. Way too freaking long. That part didn't care that this was the enemy, didn't care that she'd perpetrated a crime upon his hat. It just cared that he was a man touching her hair, a man who seemed to see past all of her artificial "lawyer" constructs—a man less than three inches from her face.

Kiss me.

He didn't. With a jerk of his head, he let her hair slip through his fingers and took an all-important step away from her. A sense of irrational rejection immediately took up battle with relief.

She wasn't out of the woods yet, though. He was still watching her every movement, her every twitch. Her footing became more familiar. She could do this, whatever *this* was. "I do not take kindly to being a target," he finally said into the wind.

"I don't know of anyone who does." She watched his face as she flipped her hair back over her shoulder. His eyes followed the movement. Why hadn't he kissed her? "If I find out anything about it, I'll let you know."

He licked his lower lip. Yes, it did appear that a beautiful woman could muddle a man's thinking. He pulled his wallet out of his back pocket and fished out a business card. "If you find out anything," he said, the sarcasm dripping off every syllable, "give me a call. I'd like to press charges. That address is wrong, but the cell number is still good."

Armstrong Holdings, the card said. Wichita Falls, Texas. Daniel Armstrong, Chief Operating Officer. Damn. He wasn't just some errand boy, he operated the whole company. Did that include the part that wanted to build the dam? "Of course," she tried to say smoothly as she tucked the card into her pocket behind her glasses. She had the feeling that pressing charges was the least of her worries. But a cell phone number wasn't exactly an in. She needed something more. "Where are you staying now?"

The steel left his eyes a little. Yes, maybe they were both back on familiar footing now, because a smaller version of that arrogant smile was back. "At my uncle's house." He slouched back against the side of his truck, one thumb caught in a belt loop, the other holding the apparently forgotten hat. Now that the anger had left his face—or at least gone deeper under cover—he was right back into handsome territory. "You should come to dinner."

"Excuse me?" Of all the things she thought he might say at that exact moment, dinner wasn't even on the list.

"Look, I can appreciate you not—" he shrugged his shoulders in defeat "—*liking* my uncle very much. But he's not such a bad guy. You should see for yourself."

The spawn of Satan wasn't *such* a bad guy? Even Dan didn't sound like he believed it. With her last bit of self-control, she managed to keep her snort to herself. Besides, a dinner invitation was exactly the sort of in she'd been angling for. Aunt Emily would be thrilled that Rosebud had managed to get invited to that creepy ranch house. God only knew what sort of dirt she could dig up from the inside.

He was falling into her trap—or, she suddenly realized, she was falling into his. After all, two could play at this game.

He notched an eyebrow at her. Oh, yes, *play* was the operative word. She mustered up her best sly grin as she pretended to think about it. "Quite the peacemaker, aren't you, Mr. Armstrong?"

"Mr. Armstrong is my uncle." His smile broadened. "Please call me Dan, Ms. Donnelly."

Suddenly, she decided she might not mind playing this game. After all, she could string him along with a wink and maybe a kiss—okay, definitely a kiss—without giving away anything, including her body. Just so long as she was the one doing the stringing. "Rosebud," she corrected him as she batted her eyes and managed a faint blush.

His smile grew warmer—she thought. "Saturday night? Around seven?"

Two days? He wasted no time. She wouldn't have the chance to find out anything about him before then. She'd be walking into the devil's lair with nothing but her wits and her looks to keep her safe. Sometimes, she thought as she carefully considered his offer, that was all a girl needed. "All right. Saturday at seven."

If she wasn't careful, that smile was going to be her undoing. "Would you like me to pick you up?"

Chivalry had apparently not died. But there was no way in hell she wanted this man in this truck to be seen picking her up on the rez. The wrong people would get the wrong idea, and she had enough to deal with right now. "I know where it is."

He nodded his head in acknowledgment, and she felt the heat from three paces. Definitely a kiss. At least one. One kiss to hold her for the next three years—was that too much to ask? "Good. I'll see you then."

She couldn't tell if it was a threat or a promise.

Four

Dan sat in his truck, fighting the urge to head straight for the barn, saddle up Smokey and head for the valley. The expectation of bad days were the whole reason he'd driven himself and his horse up here from Texas. He wasn't going to leave Smokey, his champion palomino stallion, at home—being around Cecil practically guaranteed he'd need to ride.

A bad day at the office was always made better by taking Smokey out to check on the Armstrong oil derricks. Dan paid people to make sure the derricks ran properly, but there was something about getting his own hands dirty that made him feel like the company was all his. Usually, by the time he rode back in, whatever problem that had been bugging him had either ceased to be important or a solution had presented itself. Sometimes both.

He could sure use a solution to his long list of current problems, starting with who'd fired on him. He had a feeling that if he camped out in that valley long enough, his Lakota princess would come back to the scene of the crime. He'd rather take his chances there than go in and see his uncle. Going in would mean reporting back, and reporting back would mean having to say something about Rosebud Donnelly, and saying something about Rosebud was…tricky.

He couldn't be sure, but damned if that woman hadn't looked just like his Indian princess, minus the horse. She had the nerve to do it, too. The cold-eyed determination he'd seen when he called her on it told him she had nothing but ice water running through her veins. No doubt about it, that was the bearcat Cecil wanted dealt with. She was why Dan was here. Regular lawyers couldn't budge her. He was supposed to *woo* her, for God's sake, with all his "talking." He was supposed to talk his way into her panties, compromise her position and report back.

He was no lapdog.

His princess. Somehow, he knew there was more to her than just that. Underneath all that cold determination, he'd seen something in her eyes, something that had spoken of a deep sorrow, a deep regret. Something that made him think that if she had taken that shot, she hadn't shot to kill.

He couldn't be sure. But he had a hunch, and he hadn't had one lead him astray in a long time.

But what was he supposed to do with it? Make wild accusations—the kind Rosebud was making? What the hell was that about—"Men have died"? Cecil was an ass—that much he knew—but he wasn't a killer. He didn't need to be one—it was just a dam.

Most every person has a reason, his mother's voice whispered in his ear. If ever there was a situation where his mother's sensibilities would come in handy, this was it. He turned his phone over in his hand, debating whether or not he should check in with Mom. On one hand, her opinion on these sorts of matters was worth its weight in oil. On the other hand, he'd have to tell her about the gunshot, and once he did that, she'd go all Mom on him, and she was plenty busy keeping the day-to-day operations going while he was up here dealing with the Cecil "situation." She was the reason he had time to spend days taking notes with Rosebud. Nope. He couldn't bring Mom in on this yet. He needed her focused on the meetings and deals he'd lined up before he left.

Dan thought hard, trying to review the interview as his mother would. Rosebud Donnelly's voice had cracked and Emily Mankiller had touched her, like a mother comforting her child. His first instinct—she'd lost someone, maybe a husband—had been true. Maybe Rosebud had taken a shot at him to make up for a different shot, a better shot. That had to be it.

Did that even the score? Was she satisfied? No, he decided. A woman like that was never satisfied with *just* once. He smiled at the thought. But he didn't think she was going to take another shot at him. He'd looked her in the eyes. Her mouth may have been lying, but he didn't think her eyes were telling the same tale.

No, they'd been saying something…different. He adjusted his jeans. Damn it all. He shouldn't have gotten so close to her, so close to the way she smelled, to those beautiful eyes the shade of a doe's fur in the early spring. He never should have touched her hair, one long swath of silk. He never should have shaken her hand.

For that matter, he never should have come here.

And now, he thought in resignation, he had to go in *there*. *Time to get this over with.* Dan grabbed his dead hat off the dash. He needed a new one, pronto. A man didn't go without a hat where he was from.

"Well?" Dan hadn't even made it to the door of the dining room. He sighed. There was no avoiding his uncle. The whole house stunk of him.

Dan was so busy mulling over the best way to handle telling Cecil about the situation that he didn't see the man in the black leather jacket sitting in front of Cecil until he stood up. Another Lakota Indian? What was Cecil doing with someone who sure as hell looked like one of the very people suing Armstrong Holdings?

"Dan Armstrong," he said, making the first move. A fellow could tell a lot about a person by his handshake.

"Shane Thrasher," the stranger said. His grip started out rock-hard, but quickly went limp, like he was trying to hide something. Dan decided he didn't like the man, an opinion reinforced by his uncle's warm smile for Thrasher. Nope. Didn't like him at all.

"Thrasher is—what are you, again?" Cecil opened a lockbox Dan hadn't seen before and pulled out a thick file. The box looked old—like the house. Definitely not something Cecil normally had in his office.

"Half Crow," Thrasher replied as he sat back down. He acted like he'd sat in that chair a lot.

Hadn't Emily Mankiller said something about the Crow tribe? Something about Custer and Little Bighorn and Greasy Grass? What Dan needed was an eighth-grade history book, but if he was remembering correctly, according to Ms. Mankiller, the Crow were the ones who worked with the whites against the Lakota.

"That's right. I can't keep you all straight." Dan winced at Cecil's words, even though Thrasher didn't blink. "Thrasher is my head of security. An inside man, if you will."

Head of security? Dan looked him over. More like gun for hire. The bulge at his side wasn't hard to see. Maybe Rosebud Donnelly had taken a shot at Dan, maybe she hadn't. Dan had a hunch that he needed to be more worried about Shane Thrasher than a beautiful, conflicted lawyer. "Pleasure to make your acquaintance."

A muscle above Thrasher's left eye twitched in response. It appeared the insincere feeling was mutual.

Cecil was studying a thick file. "What did you think of that Donnelly woman?"

"She's trouble." An honest assessment—but he couldn't figure out if she was the good kind or the bad kind of trouble. More than likely, she was both.

Thrasher snorted in a way that struck Dan as too familiar. Wielding a red pen, Cecil made a note in the file. "Think you can handle her?"

For the first time in his life, Dan wasn't sure if he could handle a woman. In the space of one afternoon, he'd been impressed by, furious with and turned on by Rosebud Donnelly. The combination was dangerous. "I invited her to dinner Saturday night." Cecil's eyebrows shot up. "She accepted," he added. In the space of a second, he'd seen a crack in her ice-cold lawyer front. He had the feeling that keeping her on her toes was the only way to get through to her. That, and making sure she wasn't armed. But he'd be damned if he'd bring up any of that in front of Thrasher.

"That's my boy." Cecil's grin was wide. He looked downright happy, in an evil sort of way. "What did I tell you, Thrasher?"

"You were right," Thrasher replied, the butt-kissing tone of his voice at odds with the way his face kept twitching.

Dan had the sudden urge to punch that face. Instead, he dug his fingers into the chair's armrest. "I thought it would help if she could see you as a person, not just an adversary." Although, with that grin, Dan was having trouble seeing Cecil as more than an adversary right now, too.

Cecil gave him the same look he'd been giving Dan since the day after his father's funeral—the shut-up-and-be-an-Armstrong look. "I don't give a rat's ass how she sees me. I'm not running some feel-good love-in around here. I want you to find her weak spots. I want you to bring her *down*. Understood?"

Right then, Dan wished he'd never had to leave Texas. In Texas, he ran a tight ship. Armstrong Holdings was one of the twenty best places to work in Texas, or so some award hanging in the reception area said. But the South Dakota division of Armstrong Holdings seemed to be a different can of worms, and Dan was feeling particularly slimy today. He reminded himself that Cecil's lack of ethics was the exact reason he'd come—there was no place for slime in any part of Dan's company. "She won't make me any copies of her files, but she'll let me see them to take notes."

A look that was dangerously close to victory flashed over Cecil's face. "Well, then, that's something, isn't it? I underestimated you, son."

Son. The chair creaked. Dan was in serious danger of breaking off an armrest or two. Thrasher had the nerve to snort in amusement.

"I've got a fundraiser in Sioux Falls Saturday night. It'll be just the two of you," Cecil went on as he made another note with the red pen. "I expect results."

Dan would also like to see some results—but he wanted to believe his reasons were more noble. "Interested lust" was better than "cold-blooded scheming." Wasn't it? At least Thrasher hadn't gotten this assignment. But then, Dan didn't think Thrasher would get anywhere with Rosebud. She didn't seem like the kind of woman who went for jerks.

"What about him?" Dan didn't even look at Thrasher—he was too afraid he'd lose the last of his cool and punch him.

"Don't worry your pretty little head about me," Thrasher replied as he stood, conveniently moving out of range. "In fact, I doubt you'll ever see me again, Armstrong."

Dan shot to his feet. But by the time he got turned around, Thrasher was gone. Dan swung back around, his fists ready.

"We're all on the same side here," was all Cecil said as he locked the box back up.

No, Dan didn't think they were.

He didn't know whose side he was on.

Five

Her aged, dented Taurus made it to the Armstrong ranch house. That was a good thing. And the weather wasn't so hot that she was sweating in her suit, so that was also a good thing.

But beyond those two good things, Rosebud was grasping at straws. The whole situation had an air of unreality to it. Was she really about to have dinner—at his house—with the one-and-only Cecil Armstrong? With Dan Armstrong? Was she really this scared about it?

Oh, yeah, she was terrified. If she'd owned chain mail, she would have put it on under the jacket, but she didn't, so she'd settled for a lower-cut-than-normal tank top in a soft-and-flirty pink under her gray suit. That was as close as she got to pretty when she was about to do battle.

She could do this. She was a lawyer, damn it. She'd argued a case before the South Dakota Supreme Court, for God's sake—argued and won. She could handle the Armstrong men.

She grabbed her briefcase and put on her game face. But before she could get anywhere, the front door swung open and out stepped the cowboy of her dreams.

The white, button-up shirt was cuffed to the elbows, and the belt buckle sat just so on the narrow V of his waist. For a blinding second, she hoped he'd turn around and go right back inside, just so she could see what that backside looked like without a saddle or a sports coat to block the view. She thought she saw a loaded holster at his side, but she realized it was a cell phone. All that was missing was a white horse and a sunset to ride off into.

Just one kiss, she thought as she fought to keep a satisfied smile off her face. Kissing Dan Armstrong wouldn't be the worst thing in the world, would it?

"You're right on time," Dan said as he came down to greet her. When he shook her hand this time, he acted like he was one step away from kissing it.

Maybe two kisses. Darn it, this whole situation was driving her crazy. She fought the urge to swing her briefcase in between them like it was a guillotine. "I'm sure your uncle appreciates punctuality."

Dan still had her hand. Warm, again, and still not sweaty. He wasn't nervous. The realization made *her* even more nervous. "He probably does. But he's not here."

Relief flooded her system at the same time her heartbeat picked up another notch. "Oh?" Was it just the two of them?

The look in Dan's eyes said yes, it was just the two of them. The gentle pressure his fingers were exerting on her wrist seconded the motion. "He's at some fundraiser."

She was going to have to draw the line at three kisses, tops. Any more than that, and this man would have her in a compromising position behind enemy lines. "You understand that no matter what party he tries to buy off, I'm going to do everything in my power to make sure he doesn't get elected?"

"Completely." No, there was no mistaking Dan's feelings. He didn't like his own uncle. But if that was true, what was he doing here, with her? Finally, he let go of her hand and stepped back. As his eyes skimmed her body, she saw his brow wrinkle. "This isn't a business meeting, you know."

Just her luck—he really was that observant. He'd noticed her suit—what were the odds he remembered it was the same one she'd had on two days ago? She jutted out her chin in defiance of all known fashion laws and bluffed her way past the blush she was sure she was working on. "You didn't expect me to treat this as a social call, did you?"

"No, I guess I didn't." He offered her his arm. Chivalry was not only *not* dead, it was also apparently alive and well in his part of Texas. She ignored the flattered feeling that started to hum high in her chest. So what if it had been an awfully long time since any white man had done more than look down his nose at her? She was not going to let this "respect" thing go to her head. "Shall we?"

As they walked up the porch steps, Rosebud had the distinct feeling that she was walking into the jaws of hell, and the demon house would swallow her down in one big gulp. She fought the urge to cling to Dan's arm. She wasn't some weak female who needed a male protector. It wasn't her fault if her fingers wrapped around his bare skin.

"Have you ever been here?" he said as he held the door for her.

"Never *in*. Just *by*," she said as her eyes adjusted to the darkened interior of the foyer. Actually, it looked nothing like a dungeon. Everything was neat and clean—even the mounted buffalo head she could see in the parlor was dust-free. The rooms had a warm, almost feminine sensibility to them.

He nodded as he guided her down a long, dark hallway. "To hear Maria tell it, Cecil's never set foot in any rooms but the dining room and his bedroom. I guess the rest of this place is like a museum."

"Who's Maria?"

"The housekeeper. She made us dinner tonight." Dan pushed open a swinging door. "Oh, good. Maria, meet my guest, Rosebud Donnelly, the Lakota lawyer who's suing Cecil. Rosebud, this is Maria Villerreal. She basically runs the place." His tongue rolled the *R*s right. She flushed hot, thinking of his tongue rolling anything.

"Señor!" Maria was a small woman with a thick accent who was in the middle of putting on her coat. She ducked her head to Rosebud. "It is an honor to meet you, *señorita.*"

"The pleasure is mine." Again, this was not what she expected. A pristine mansion and kindly hired help? Maybe she had Cecil Armstrong all wrong.

"Dinner is in the oven, *señor.* Do you need anything else?"

Dan patted her arm, and Rosebud saw the girlish blush rise up. "No, Maria, it smells wonderful. You can head out—give my best to Eduardo and the boys, okay?"

"Sí, señor." Maria held out her hand to Rosebud. "Señor Daniel is a good man, *señorita.*"

As opposed to…his uncle? The statement opened the door to about twenty questions. Dan couldn't have been around that long, or she would have heard about his arrival *before* he showed up at her office. How long had Maria worked for Cecil? Clearly, Dan was working his charm on more people than her. That wasn't a bad thing, either, she decided. This wasn't any different than judging a date by how he treated the waiter—except, she reminded herself, this wasn't a date. Now that Maria was out of the house, Rosebud had to remember that.

Dan pulled out a stool at the huge kitchen island and motioned for her to sit. She felt a little silly about the formality, but she couldn't say no to that smile. "We're eating in the kitchen?"

"The dining room is Cecil's headquarters." Dan got busy with plates and forks before he opened the oven. The scent of Mexican—good Mexican—filled the air. "The kitchen is a much nicer place, trust me. I hope you like tamales."

Sounded like the dining room was the place she needed to be. Something occurred to her. "You call him Cecil?"

Dan paused, a sheepish smile on his face. "Yeah, I guess I do."

"You don't like him very much, do you?"

"Not many people do." He dug out some cheese and proceeded to garnish the tamales. *A good-looking man who knows how to garnish,* Rosebud thought in amazement. *No,* she caught herself. She would *not* be impressed. "You don't like him."

That was putting it mildly. "I've never actually met him. He's *your* uncle."

"And there's not a damn thing I can do about that." He sounded lighthearted, but the tension in his voice was unmistakable as he set her dinner before her. "I'd offer you a beer, but that suit says I'd be wasting my breath." Here, just the two of them in a kitchen that smelled of warmth and goodness, she allowed herself to smile. His eyes latched on to her smile, and she froze. Did he think he recognized her from the valley? Or was he just staring? "Lemonade?" he finally said into the silence.

Disaster averted, she thought with a mental sigh. "I'd love some."

"Tell me about your name." He set the lemonade down in front of her, but he didn't withdraw. Instead, he stood in the space between touching her shoulder and not touching her shoulder.

She looked up. No, there wasn't any of that wariness she

thought she'd caught a glimpse of. His eyes weren't so stormy, she decided. They were more like the palest jade with just a hint of gray. A precious stone. "Is that the nice way of asking if I'm named after a sled?"

Jade probably didn't sparkle as much as Dan's eyes. "My mother loves *Citizen Kane*," he said and then headed back to the stove to scoop out Spanish rice. "I bet you get that question a lot."

Her mouth watered. Whatever else happened tonight, at least the food was going to be good. "Only from white people."

His shoulders shook with laughter. "Guilty as charged."

At least he had a sense of humor about it. That was a rare thing in and of itself, especially considering the past three years. She was used to dealing with *that man's* lawyers, who held her in obvious contempt. When she was in college, she'd become familiar with white people who had an overdeveloped sense of liberal guilt. And the locals? They mostly treated her—or any Indian, for that matter—like dirty, dumb Injuns. Dan didn't fit into any of those categories. "You don't have to be all politically correct, either—*Indian* is fine. I think of myself as a Lakota Indian."

He regarded her with a look that was between frank curiosity and open respect. "Duly noted. So are you named after a sled?"

She couldn't help but grin widely at him. "I'm named after a distant relative who moved to New York in the '40s, Rosebud Yellow Robe. Family legend is that Orson Welles named the sled after her—they both did radio shows for CBS back in the day."

"Interesting." His voice dropped a notch as he served dinner with a flourish. "And the Donnelly?"

She wasn't much of a cook, and this was, hands down, the most delicious meal she'd had in ages. She forced herself to focus. If she wasn't mistaken, that was a pretty slick way of asking if Donnelly was her maiden or married name. "A grandmother married a white man after the Civil War, and they had nothing but sons for a while."

"Until you."

She froze, the fork halfway to her mouth. Her appetite disappeared, leaving only uneasiness in her belly. Carefully, she lowered the fork back to the plate and cleared her throat. "I had a brother. He was one of the deaths deemed a suicide by the FBI."

Out of the corner of her eye, she saw his hand flex. *Way to go,* Rosebud scolded herself. Way to play the pity card. *Way to use Tanner's memory.* Suddenly, she felt dirty. This whole situation was wrong. There had to be better ways to get to Cecil Armstrong. If she thought real hard, she was sure she could come up with *something.* Anything would be better than this intimate dinner with his nephew.

He finally spoke into the silence. "I'm goin' to look into it."

"You said that." She tried to shrug this whole awkward conversation off but failed miserably.

He pivoted on his stool, put a hand on her shoulder and turned her to face him. "I mean it."

She wanted to believe him, but she'd had too many men—white and Indian—break too many promises. Still, something about the way he met her gaze made her think that maybe, just maybe, this time would be different.

She was getting warmer. Just like when he'd shaken her hand, she could feel the slow burn moving from where he was touching her shoulder down her arm and across her chest. Despite the confusion that swirled in her head, she still felt the pull of sexual tension. She tested out a small smile and got an honest one in return as his hand drifted down to her arm and gave it a little squeeze. That burn got a lot less slow.

Oh, boy. If she wasn't careful, all this promising and smiling and touching would pull her right under. She was already a mess right now. She couldn't afford something as distracting as sexual tension to further unscrew her head. "A man of his word?"

"Always." His fingers trailed down her arm, leaving scorch marks under her jacket. He motioned to the food. "It's goin' to get cold."

Luckily, dinner was still warm—and delicious. Eating it gave her a little time to get her thoughts organized, because the last thing she wanted to do was add the embarrassment of spewing half-chewed tamales across the kitchen island. Finally, the plates were nearly empty and she'd moved on to the lemonade. She decided to start with the least dangerous topic she could think of. "You'll have to tell Maria that I said this was wonderful."

"She'll like that."

"How long have you known her?"

"About a week."

Okay, that answered her question about how long he'd been here. No wonder she hadn't heard about his arrival. "Really? You seem like old friends."

Maybe that grin wasn't arrogant. Maybe that grin was just confident. "My mother raised me to be nice to everyone, regardless of whether they were the maid or the king of the world." Then the grin slid right on over into arrogant. "Plus, I gave Maria a—what do they call it these days? A retention bonus. My uncle was still paying her the same wage he hired her at five years ago."

That didn't surprise her. "Your mother sounds like a wise woman," she said, hoping she was using the right tense.

"She is. She's the executive vice president. We run the Texas division of the company as a team—before this thing with Cecil pulled me up here, that is." He began to rummage through the fridge. "I think Maria left a cake—interested?"

"Yes, please. Will your mother be visiting you here?" Because she'd kind of like to meet the woman who produced this charmer.

"She wouldn't be caught dead in the same state as Cecil."

It was interesting to watch him drift between hot and serious, chatty and silent. Dan didn't exactly wear his heart on his sleeve, but she got the feeling he didn't win a lot of poker games. "Sounds like a long story."

"It's not so much long as it is old. Mom picked Dad instead of Cecil. Cecil never forgave either of them. He didn't even come to Dad's funeral."

"And you work for him?" It was out of her mouth before she could stop it.

Dan set a piece of cake in front of her, pulled up his stool and sat down. Only then did he turn to her, his eyes going right past serious and straight on over into dangerous. She wondered if other people made him look this dangerous, or if it was just her. "Let's get something straight," he said, sounding very much like a man who would take all comers. "I don't work *for* Cecil. I inherited my father's stake in the family business. I own half of this house, the water rights and the dam project. This is my company just as much as it is his."

That nerve she'd hit was *huge.* She wondered if Cecil had the same interpretation of the situation. "But you're helping him."

He glared at her. All the charm was gone. "I'm *helping* my company."

She had pushed this just about as far as she could, but she couldn't quit. This was her in—Dan didn't like his uncle, and he didn't like the job the old man was doing. The chance that she could convince Dan to abandon the whole thing was small, but it was a chance she had to take. "Well, *your* company is going to flood *my* reservation."

He looked away, like she'd won and he'd lost. But then he said, "Eminent domain."

So he'd been doing his homework, and they both knew who the loser here was going to be. The government would give the reservation to Cecil because lower electricity rates were good for politicians and their reelections. It was a new twist on the old story—the white people needed the land more than the Indians did. And yet, she felt like she needed to comfort him. He actually looked miserable about the whole damn thing. Leaning over, she touched one of those forearms and said, "I won't go down without a fight."

Moving slowly, he set his fork down and took her fingers in his hand. Calluses rubbed against the length of her index finger, then moved on to her palm. If she hadn't been sitting, her knees would have buckled. "I'm counting on that." Oh, that wasn't a threat—that was a promise, pure and simple. "But the question is, what kind of fight?"

She couldn't help it. Three long years of loneliness threatened to swamp her altogether. She leaned into him, close enough that she could see a faint scar above his cheek, close enough that his short hair could tickle her nose. "You can check my briefcase. I don't have a gun."

He turned to her as he pulled her hand into his rock-solid chest. "Not here, anyway," he murmured as his lips brushed hers. "You're too smart for that."

Huh? *She* was smart? She was the one sitting in Cecil Armstrong's kitchen, kissing Cecil Armstrong's nephew—a man she barely knew, a man she'd shot at, for God's sake!

But how was he being any smarter? He knew—or thought he knew—that she'd put a hole in his hat, less than two inches from his skull! What kind of man came on to a woman he believed to be armed and dangerous? What kind of man worked for—with—Cecil Armstrong? What kind of man *was* Dan Armstrong?

Oh. My. God. The kissing kind, that's what.

His touch wasn't an act of aggression or domination, but more like he was asking for permission. Not the kiss of an enemy, but of something…different. Even though his fingers tightened around hers, he hung back, waiting for a sign. His other hand came up and stroked her cheek with the lightest of touches. Tension—the good sort—hit her like a small jolt of electricity, pushing her into him. That must have been what he was waiting for, because his tongue brushed her lips, and she forgot all about being smart. Instead, she remembered being a woman, remembered the feeling of desire as it surged from her mouth, flamed to her breasts and scorched down farther until she wanted nothing more than to see exactly how far this kiss could go.

Six

He really hadn't meant to kiss her—not before dessert, anyway. But she'd touched him, and promised that she'd fight him every single step of the way. The way she'd said it.... She'd said it not like she was about to serve him a subpoena, but like she was suggesting they continue their discussion in bed.

He was supposed to be getting to her, breaking down her defenses, finding her weak spots and exploiting them. But that wasn't what was happening.

What was happening was that she was getting to him.

He couldn't give less of a damn about whatever business pretense he'd used to get her here. What mattered was that she was here, now, kissing him. He wanted to taste more of her. Hell, he wanted to taste all of her. She had a honeyed sweetness that was tempered with a hint of tart lemonade. Her fingers tightened around his shirt, pulling him into her. She opened her lips for him, and he felt her jolt when his tongue touched hers. For a second, he knew he was about to get lucky. His body was aching for it, too.

Then, suddenly, he was puckering up to nothing but air. She jerked back, yanking her hand away from his chest so hard that she just about took his shirt with her—but not in the fun way.

What the hell? She went right past a pretty pink and straight on over to hit-with-a-tomato red, her eyes fastened on the forgotten cake in front of them. Just as much as her hands and her mouth had been telling him "yes" a second before, the rest of her was screaming "no," loud and clear. The buzzy hard-on he'd been working on slammed right back up into his gut. Gritting his teeth, he tried to get his eyes to focus. It didn't help. She looked more miserable than a woman he'd been kissing ought to.

And that cold shoulder she was giving him said nothing but *mistake* and *regret*. It left a bad taste in his mouth that had nothing to do with the lip-lock. "I shouldn't have done that," he offered. It sounded weak, even to his own ears.

She jumped at the words and was off the stool before he knew what was happening. "I should go." Her eyes cut back to him. The softness there was disappearing faster than a puddle in August. "Now."

No use arguing with that. She'd made up her mind, that much was clear. "I'll walk you to your car."

She didn't offer any resistance, but she made sure to keep her distance from him as she stomped down the hall, out the front door and into a deepening dusk. It was only when she got to the gate that she pulled up. "Thank you for dinner." She put both hands behind her back. "Please tell Maria I enjoyed the food."

Just the food? Ouch. The woman's claws were razor sharp. "I'm still coming by your office Monday at nine." Even though the dusk was settling, he could see the flash of anger in her eyes. But she'd said it herself—he was a man of his word, and he needed to know more about her brother before he started digging around. "If it's all right with you."

She let the question hang for a long moment without so much as a blink. No wonder Cecil had already gone through three lawyers. A pissed Rosebud Donnelly was an intimidating Rosebud Donnelly. His eyes darted back to her ugly little car, but thankfully he saw no gun propped up against the window or anything.

"Of course," she finally said, her chin jutting out in a way that said it was anything but okay with her. "You're just doing your job."

Once she was in her car, the rear tires spun out on the gravel before she got enough traction to peel out, but her words hung around. *Just doing his job.*

He felt lower than a rattler's belly in a wagon rut, all because he was *just doing his job.*

As he turned to go back into the house, an orange light caught his eyes. Just a small dot of bright color that had no business being about six feet off the ground behind some bushes. As quick as he'd seen it, it was gone. He couldn't see anything else amiss.

The hairs stood up on the back of his neck. *"In fact,"* Thrasher's voice sneered in his ear, *"I doubt you'll ever see me again."*

His uncle was having him watched. A deep rage threatened to break free, the same rage he'd felt shortly after Dad had died, when his uncle had showed up and informed Mom that if she didn't marry him, he'd take the company away from her. Dan had only been sixteen at the time. He hadn't let Cecil call the shots then—he and Mom had gotten enough stock to keep the board firmly on their side—and he sure as hell wasn't going to let Cecil call the shots now.

Screw it, Dan thought, forcing himself to walk calmly back into the house. No need to let Thrasher know Dan suspected anything. *Screw Cecil Armstrong. Screw this whole job.*

Except for the kiss.

Dan had just one thing he *could* do. He spent the rest of his Saturday night taking the kitchen apart, looking for hidden cameras and microphones.

He knew whose side he was on.

"Good morning, Mr. Armstrong."

Dan didn't even have one foot in the door, and already the receptionist was coming at him with a cup of coffee. Today, he was going to hold steady at two cups, max. "Ms. Donnelly is waiting for you."

"Thank you...Judy." Her friendly smile told him he'd gotten that right.

She led him back to the sorriest excuse for a conference room he'd ever been in. To his surprise, Rosebud was already settled in with a banker's box of files in front of her. "Good morning, Mr. Armstrong." She didn't even look up. "You're on time."

She sounded exactly like the receptionist and nothing like a woman he'd kissed two nights ago. "Rosebud." To heck with this *mister* and *miz* stuff. "I thought you would appreciate punctuality."

That got her to look up, and even earned him a small smile. Man, how did she manage to shine in a room this ugly? The walls were the color of overcooked oatmeal, and he thought he deserved a buckle for managing to make the eight seconds on that chair last time.

As quick as that smile had shown up, it disappeared again. He wondered if she had a gun in her briefcase. "Are these your files?"

"Not all of them." He leaned over to try and see what she was writing, but she caught him and flipped the top sheet back over the one she'd made notes on. "But this is more than enough to keep you busy for today."

Dan looked around and was surprised to see that the two extra chairs had disappeared. He'd have to sit in that craptastic chair again. He had to hand it to Rosebud. She didn't have a lot to work with, but she made the most of it. "Which files are these?"

"What do you mean?"

"Cecil files, dam files or police files?"

No reaction this time. He had his work cut out for him today. Right now, not only was Rosebud *not* a woman who invited a touch or a kiss, but she wasn't exactly leaving any of her weak spots out in the open. "Police files." She turned her attention back to her own notes. "You are a man of your word, after all."

"Yes, ma'am." Moving cautiously, he lowered himself into the evil chair. It promptly let out a muffled squeak, like he'd sat on a squirrel—or worse. He glanced up to see the amusement on her face. "Enjoyin' yourself?"

"Immensely."

So she was laughing at him. The difference between Rosebud scowling and Rosebud smiling was worth sounding like he'd eaten nothing but chili for the last month. He pulled the top file and started reading the first police report.

Tanner Donnelly, male, age twenty-eight when he was found by his aunt, Emily Mankiller, with a .22 in his hand and the matching slug in his temple four years ago. Survived by his aunt and his sister, Rosebud. The file noted that the women claimed Donnelly's dog tags were missing, but the investigators could find no trace of them.

The FBI agent in charge had been Thomas Yellow Bird. Rosebud had a separate file on Yellow Bird—seemed he was an acquaintance of Tanner Donnelly and had pushed the investigation as far as his supervisors would let him. There was also a log of emails and phone calls with a James Carlson, who was a federal prosecutor in D.C.

Something didn't add up, Dan thought as he wrote the name down. A guy named Yellow Bird he could understand, but Rosebud had D.C. contacts? Well, maybe not. The last date she'd written down was over ten months ago. She must have hit a brick wall—which was why she was asking *him* for help, of all people.

In addition to police and FBI files, there was a thick file of notes and interviews, some typed and some handwritten in a delicate script. Handwritten? This whole thing just got odder and odder, but he pressed on, copying down every possibly relevant piece of information. His hand began to cramp. He didn't normally like those little computers—too easy to drop—but he was thinking maybe he'd pick one up the next time he was in town.

By the time he finished, Dan was pretty sure he knew everything about Tanner Donnelly, from what kind of cereal he ate for breakfast to the name of the first girl he'd ever kissed. Seemed like a decent guy. If Rosebud's notes were accurate— and he had no reason to doubt that—then he could see how she refused to accept the suicide ruling.

But he'd seen no red flags, nothing that said Cecil or even Thrasher. Not even a casual connection to Armstrong Holdings.

He had nothing.

When he leaned back to rub his eyes, he found Rosebud watching him. "Well?"

"You're nothing if not thorough."

She cocked her head to one side and bounced the end of her pen on the table. Dan had the distinct feeling he was about to be cross-examined. "Is that what you told your uncle?"

"Beg pardon?"

"When you reported back about our evening. I'm sure he was…curious, shall we say, to know if you accomplished your assignment."

He might be mistaken, but he thought he saw a little bit of that pink come back into her cheeks. "Are you asking me if I told him I kissed you?"

He wasn't mistaken. The pink got prettier as her eyes cut to the doorway, but it was empty. "That was your assignment, wasn't it? I'm not stupid, Mr. Armstrong."

She had him dead to rights. He really hoped she didn't have a gun in that briefcase. "Only a fool would assume you were." Because it sure would be nice to know she didn't think him a total idiot—or worse, Cecil's lapdog.

She smirked at the compliment, but didn't return the favor. "You're avoiding the question."

He couldn't tell which part of her was doing damage control, the lawyer or the woman. "You act like my company kissed your tribe."

For a second, he saw a little bit of doubt on her face. "Wasn't that the point?"

He knew the chair might kill him, but he took the chance and leaned forward—not close enough to touch her, but close enough that he could tell she was biting the inside of her lip. The chair whined pitifully, but at least it held. "Did it ever occur to you that *I* was kissin' *you?*"

Oh, she was tough. Aside from that lovely blush she was working on, she didn't react at all—not even to lean away from him. "Does your uncle see such a distinction?"

Which was a nice, polite way of saying "answer the damn question." He shook his head, hoping his amusement didn't further piss her off. "You want to know what I told him?"

"Please." She sat up a little straighter.

Dan looked at her for a few more seconds before he hazarded leaning back in his chair. If Cecil heard what he was about to say, he'd draw and quarter Dan for treason. But the search for bugs in the kitchen had turned up nothing, as had the search of his room. He was going on a hope and a prayer that this room wasn't bugged. "I told him that you were tougher than I thought. I told him you couldn't be wined and dined. I told him I'd need more time."

She was silent. Her pretty blush drained away, but that was the only sign she'd heard him. "I see. Did you give him an idea of how much time you'd need?"

Hell, he was in this far. "He told me the next court date is in five weeks." Besides, she'd said so herself. She wasn't stupid.

"Let me guess. He wants me out of the picture before then." Her voice had a new, pinched tone to it.

"That's what *he* wants."

A stillness came over her. Her pen didn't bounce, her eyes didn't blink and he couldn't tell without staring, but he was reasonably confident that her chest didn't even rise. When she did speak, it came out as a whisper. A pained whisper. "What do *you* want?"

Which was a hell of a good question. But he wasn't going to come up with an answer sitting in this demon chair. He got up as smoothly as he could and went to the window. She needed a moment to get herself together, he rationalized. "You know Google? The company motto is 'Don't be evil.'"

She snorted behind his back. "That's noble, but naive."

"No, dinner was noble but naive," he shot back.

"I'm *not* naive."

"Not you. Me." Because thinking he could walk the line between "interested lust" and "cold-blooded scheming" was obviously one of his dumber ideas. And to expect her to believe him? He turned back to her. "It was naive of me to think that me kissin' you could be a separate…thing from your tribe suing my company." So much for being good at talking.

Even sitting in judgment of him, she was beautiful. What he wanted was to ask her out on a real date, to take her someplace far away from this crappy conference room and Cecil's ranch house, someplace where it wasn't Armstrong Holdings talking to the Red Creek Tribe, but just Dan and Rosebud. He'd love to get her hair out of that braid, get her out of that... For the first time, he noticed her suit. It looked like the same one she'd worn to dinner—and the same one she'd had on last week.

She only had one suit?

He must have been staring, because she began gathering up files. The movement did little to hide the embarrassment on her face.

"What happened to your copier?" The question was out before he knew where it came from. Somehow, he knew the answer was connected to a lawyer that only owned one suit.

He could see the tension ripple along her shoulders. "It's broken." She hefted the banker's box and made a break for the door. "Good day, Mr. Armstrong."

The door shut behind her.

As Dan's eyes adjusted to the bright sunlight in the parking lot, he noticed the man immediately. The black Crown Victoria, the full-wrap sunglasses and the black suit were hard to miss in this heat. Some kind of law was trying mighty hard to look casual in the middle of the parking lot at four in the afternoon.

The guy looked a little like a Lakota Indian—right color, but wrong everything else. His hair was short and that suit probably set him back a cool grand. Not the local police. And the man was watching him behind those glasses. Dan could tell by the way his chin moved.

This place must be throwing him for a loop because right now, Dan felt like he was walking into a trap and he wished with all his might he had his gun.

"Dan Armstrong?"

"Depends. Who's askin'?" Yep. Old-timey talk was just pouring out of him.

"Tom Yellow Bird." He stuck out his hand, his jacket flashing open to reveal a Glock.

Good grip, Dan thought. Not a grip of dominance, but there wasn't an ounce of weakness in the man. "What can I do for you, Mr. Yellow Bird?"

Yellow Bird gave him the once-over. "Depends on what you're doing here. Heard you were looking into the Donnelly suicide."

"Word gets around."

"It's a small rez. Going to get a lot smaller if Cecil Armstrong gets his way." Yellow Bird waited, but Dan was in no hurry to set the man's mind at ease. Yellow Bird broke first. "You've met Rosebud?"

"I have. You know her?"

"Knew her brother." The way he said it made it sound like he considered Rosebud to be the pesky little sister—always had, always would. For some reason, that made Dan want to smile—but he didn't. "We lost a good one in him."

The *we* said Indian first, FBI second. "You don't buy the suicide ruling?"

Yellow Bird scratched his throat. "Officially, that's what happened. The case has been closed for two years."

"Unofficially?"

Yellow Bird smirked, which gave his face a hard edge. Not a man to be taken lightly, that much was certain. "You know that by this time next year, where we're standing will be under about ten feet of water?"

Unofficially, Yellow Bird was still on the case. "I'm aware that that's the current plan."

"Things can always change." Yellow Bird pulled a card out of his jacket. "Unofficially."

Dan watched as the Crown Victoria pulled away, then did a slow circle to see if anyone else had witnessed the meeting. The lot was still empty, and he didn't see any faces at the narrow windows.

What the hell had that been about? For some reason, the conversation had struck Dan as being less about Tanner Donnelly and more about Armstrong Holdings. If he didn't know any better, he would have sworn that, unofficially, Yellow Bird was leaving a door open, just in case.

Damn hunches. Dan had no idea if this one was right.

As far as Rosebud was concerned, the rest of the week was simultaneously better and worse than that first meeting with Dan. He showed up at nine each morning, sat in the wobbly chair and took notes while Rosebud reviewed her case for the upcoming hearing on the preliminary injunction against the dam construction. It should have been boring, dry work, but it wasn't.

On Tuesday, Dan brought homemade chocolate-chip cookies. Wednesday was brownies and Thursday was cupcakes for the whole office. By Friday, he knew the names of everyone in the building and brought in extra cinnamon rolls for Rosebud to take to Aunt Emily. She couldn't tell if he was just buttering them—her—up or if he'd been doing his homework and knew that bringing gifts was a Lakota custom, but either way, it seemed to be working.

Judy was officially crushing on the man, and Rosebud couldn't blame her. He was easy on the eyes, smart as a whip, quite possibly richer than sin and just all around thoughtful. Add in the fact that not only did he not wear a ring, but he didn't even have the telltale faint tan lines. And one thing was certain: Dan Armstrong was eminently crushable.

Rosebud kept her defenses up, but she got the feeling that was a waste of energy. Dan was nothing if not a gentleman. He didn't make another attempt to touch her, much less kiss her. He didn't even bring up that kiss again. Instead, he did a reasonably good job of acting like the whole thing had never even happened. Conversation was kept strictly to the facts of the matter, and the fact was, he seemed to believe her about Tanner.

She decided that he'd been telling the truth—or something close to it—about keeping that kiss from his uncle. That should have made her happy. As much as she'd enjoyed it, she just couldn't bring herself to throw her body at the man, and it was clear he wasn't asking her to. He was a gentleman of the highest order.

Except that she was having dreams about that kiss—and more. In the dreams, the kiss was just the beginning. One night, they went riding and wound up a tangled mess of naked arms and legs on the banks of the Dakota. The next, an old-fashioned tepee hid them from the world. She was waking up hot and all kinds of bothered, only to have to ignore everything she actually liked about Dan to go to work. By Friday, she was officially irritated with the whole situation.

At least she wouldn't have to see him this weekend. Assuming her car could get her there in one piece, she was going to drive to her alma mater, the University of South Dakota. She needed to find out a hell of a lot more about Dan Armstrong, and she needed a computer with internet access to do it.

She only had four weeks left.

Seven

Dan stood over the huge architectural drawing, comparing the plans on the blue sheet to the engineering report. Virgil Naylor, the chief of Naylor Engineering, hovered behind him, pointing out the details. Naylor was a slight, nervous man, no doubt made all the more nervous by Dan's silence.

Something about the engineering report didn't add up, but he was having a hell of a time nailing Naylor down. He flipped to a footnote in the middle of the report. "But you say here that a run-of-river dam would generate almost as many megawatts."

"Given optimum conditions." Naylor's hands fluttered as he waved the suggestion away.

"Yes, given. So why aren't we doing a run-of-river dam?" Because that would make the most sense. A run-of-river dam wouldn't flood that pretty little valley or any significant part of the Red Creek reservation.

Naylor's mouth puckered like he was sucking on a lemon.

"Because run-of-river dams cannot store any electricity for slow times."

"And the cost benefit of that storage is?"

Naylor seemed to get a shade pinker. The effect was not a pretty one. "Over the life of the dam, it averages out to a .019 cent gain per kilowatt."

Dan stared at the man in surprise. "With a peak operating capacity of 150 megawatts?"

"Yes." Naylor snapped the word off.

Dan did the math. "That's a difference of less than three thousand dollars a year."

"Mr. Armstrong, I'm sure you can understand the advantages of long-term hydroelectric storage…" Naylor launched into all the reasons why it was best, for the third time in the last two hours.

Hell of a way to spend a Saturday, Dan thought in increasing frustration. He wondered if he could get Jim Evans, his engineer down in Amarillo, up here to look over this mess. Just then, his phone buzzed. *Thank God,* he thought as he unsnapped it from the holster. He didn't recognize the number, but it was a South Dakota area code. "Hello?"

"Dan? This is Rosebud. Donnelly," she added, like he knew tons of Rosebuds.

She was calling him. All those cookies must have worked. Dan ordered his face not to smile as he excused himself and hurried outside, away from any prying ears. "Hey. What's up?" Sheesh, what was he—thirteen again?

"Um, well, I'm…well, I'm stuck." She sounded thoroughly miserable about it. "My car died, and no one else can come get me. I need help."

A damsel in distress. And she was calling him. She was either really desperate or…well, no use getting ahead of himself. "I'm just finishing up a meeting. Where are you?"

He thought the call had been dropped, but finally she said, "Do you know where the University of South Dakota is?"

"No. Why are you at a university?"

"Um…research. Can you pick me up or not?"

The damsel was really desperate, it seemed. "Give me fifteen minutes to finish this meeting."

"I'm in parking lot D, behind the library. You should get here in an hour."

"Then I'll be seein' you in an hour." He ended the call and stared at the phone. Research? Did the university even have a law library?

"Mr. Armstrong?" Naylor hovered his way out onto the porch. "It's getting late. Do you have any other questions?"

"Just one." It took a second to get his brain off Rosebud waiting for him and back onto engineering reports. "Who else have you told about the run-of-river option?"

The man turned positively red, which was an ugly shade on his sallow skin. "I assure you that all the work at Naylor Engineering remains completely confidential at all times. We take client privileges—"

Dan cut him off with a wave of his hand. "You haven't told any of the members of the Red Creek tribe?"

"Certainly not." Naylor actually stamped his foot on the porch, looking for all the world like an indignant parakeet. "And those—those—those *savages* destroyed several thousands of dollars' worth of equipment. I wouldn't be caught dead anywhere near the lot of them."

The little man sounded just like his uncle. Dan hadn't gotten out much around here—just making the rounds between the rez, the ranch house and the dam site. Did everyone here talk like that? Was that why Rosebud had shut down that kiss so quickly—she was afraid he'd call her a savage?

He knew better. Compared to this wart with an engineering degree? Dan had no doubt that Rosebud could fit in anywhere from a honky-tonk to the boardroom to one of those garden parties Mom was fond of having in the summer. As he watched the little man get into his sedan, he knew who the real savage was—and it wasn't the pretty lawyer.

By the time he found parking lot D, it had taken him almost an hour and a half. *Damn GPS,* he grumbled to himself as he kept an eye out for an old car and a young woman. He could track the value of the euro versus the yen from up in the saddle, no wires required, but with this GPS, left versus right turns seemed to be beyond the stupid thing. It was almost five o'clock on a Saturday night, and the campus was nearly deserted. There was Rosebud's old car, parked at the far end of the lot. He didn't see her—until he pulled into the parking space.

She was sitting in the driver's seat, a white-knuckle grip on the steering wheel. Her hair was long and loose, and she was wearing a pale green T-shirt that was wonderfully snug. She almost looked like a college student instead of a top-notch legal eagle.

When she saw him, she hopped out of the car, her eyes darting around. What was she so afraid of? But that thought was arrested by the sight of Rosebud stretching herself out. Dan decided that, no matter what came out of this evening, it was all worth seeing her in that particular pair of jeans, held tight to her hips with a respectable-looking buckle.

He took it back. College girls never looked as good as she did.

"Hi," she said with a careful smile. Her eyes darted up, and her grin grew. "Nice hat."

Dan tipped the new beaver-fur felt at her. "Thanks. I'm hoping to keep this one hole-free for at least a few days."

She tilted her head to one side, and all that black silk she called hair tipped over her shoulder. His mind immediately pulled up a memory from that first ride in the valley.

It had to have been her. Sure, he'd heard some clueless idiots in the town outside the reservation claiming that all Indians looked alike, but no one else looked at him like she did. Again, he wondered what the hell her reason was. Most everybody had a reason, after all. His eyes darted down to the passenger seat. He didn't see any gun-shaped lumps—but there was a lot of glove-box room. "I'm still asking around." She was less than convincing, almost like she was tired of the lie.

Dan let it slide. It was Saturday night in what passed as a big town in this state, and he was officially in the company of a beautiful, if slightly dangerous, woman. "You didn't have to wait in the car. It's a nice night out."

She gave him a look he couldn't read. "Safer that way. The library's already closed." Before he could ask her what that was supposed to mean, she visibly shook herself and favored him with a sweet, almost shy smile. "Thanks for coming."

"What's the problem with your car?"

The weariness he thought he'd heard in her voice spread to her eyes. "It refused to start. It sounded a little funny on the drive down, but I thought it might at least get me home."

After she popped the hood, Dan poked around. He'd taken an engine or two apart in his time, but this thing was a dinosaur. The verdict wasn't good. He could see one belt in pieces and another that looked like it could go at any time. When he had Rosebud try to turn over the engine, the whole thing clicked. The starter sounded deader than a doornail and he was pretty sure the battery was corroded to the car. "When was the last time you had this thing checked out?"

She shrugged, but he noticed that she bit her lip. That was her tell. "A few years ago."

"Years?" He shook his head at her, and she managed to look sheepish. "You're probably lucky you got here."

She stuck out her chin, a move he recognized as defiance now. But she also stuck her hands into her back pockets, which emphasized her chest. "I'm lucky you were able to come get me."

Dan had long prided himself on reading the signals from the opposite sex, and he'd be damned if that particular signal didn't say "Saturday night on the town." "I guess we're both lucky, aren't we?"

Her gaze took its time working over him. By the time she got back to his face, he was working with a whole different definition of *lucky*. "That remains to be seen." He swore she purred it.

He might never figure this woman out, but he was going to have a fine time trying. "Did you call a tow truck yet?"

That was the wrong thing to say. All that goodness she'd been telegraphing his way died. "No."

"Why not?"

She was right back to looking embarrassed, and he hadn't even kissed her. Yet. "Joe can tow it home for me."

"When?" She didn't answer, which was answer enough. This hunk of steel might be here for days before someone towed it—and chances were it would be towed to the impound lot. He got his cell phone out and punched up an entry. "I've got Triple A."

"No!" She moved lightning-fast. Before he could react, her hand was on his wrist. "I mean...please."

Her touch was light, but she had a hell of a grip. That was not a bad thing. "Give me one good reason."

He prayed she couldn't feel his blood pumping as he looked down into her eyes. Then she batted her eyelashes, and he stopped caring about his pulse. "I haven't allocated the funds for a situation such as this."

Allocated the funds? It took a second for him to translate that statement to English. "You don't have the money to fix your car?"

She dropped his wrist like it was a hot potato and backed away from him, looking for all the world like a cornered animal. "No, okay? I don't have the money."

A broken copier. One suit. Handwritten notes. Driving an hour south to do "research."

She had no money. Period. A true damsel in distress.

To hell with this. It only took a second before he knew what he had to do. He began to dial. "Actually, you do." She spun on her heels, looking all sorts of angry. He held up a hand before she could let loose on him. "I've been taking up a lot of your time. My lawyer in Texas charges a hundred and twenty-five dollars an hour for consulting. Figure, what? Six hours a day for five days? That's about four thousand."

Her jaw dropped. "Dollars?"

"Yup."

"I can't—"

A voice crackled over the phone. "Yeah, I need a tow to a repair shop."

By the time he got off the phone, Rosebud was sitting on the curb, her knees tucked up under her chin. She didn't look happy about being rescued. Instead, she looked nervous. Trapped.

Dan sat down next to her. "Will you believe me if I tell you that no one knows I'm here?"

She shrugged, making sure to keep a solid eight inches between them. "Should I?"

"You might consider the option, as it happens to be the truth."

He caught the corner of her smile in his peripheral vision. Took a lot of work not to stare. "I'm a lawyer, Dan. The truth is highly relative."

"I'm more of a black-and-white guy, myself. My mom always said to be up front about the black and white because it makes lyin' about the gray a hell of a lot easier." She snorted in what he hoped was appreciation. "The fact of the matter is that I told no one about the kiss. After you left, I checked the kitchen for bugs and came up empty. Today, I took your call outside where no one could hear me, and told no one—not even Maria—who called or where I was going."

Her head nodded as she thought about it. Thinking was progress. "So what's the gray area here?"

Dan looked out. The summer sun was just scooting behind some of the taller buildings, throwing cozy shadows over the parking lot. "I'm going to be hungry by the time we get out of here. We're going to stop somewhere and get dinner, and I'm buying."

She was on her feet, backing away from him. Cornered, he thought again. "I can't—"

He climbed to his feet and took a chance by taking her hand. She didn't pull away—yet—but her hand was like a bar of steel. "You can, and you will. The gray area is that I'd like to call it a date—a date between you and me," he hurried to add when she tried to yank her hand away. This was not going as well as he wanted it to. "I'd like it to stay between you and me. No uncles, no aunts, no corporations, no tribes."

"What if I say no?"

"You wouldn't be the first." It had been close to a year since he'd parted ways with his last lady friend. There wasn't anyone left in Wichita Falls who was interested in him instead of his money. He was usually too busy to try to make the Fort Worth social scene anymore. But he still managed to have a few dates every now and then. She wouldn't be the first, and she wouldn't be the last.

She was chewing on the inside of her lip again. Thinking was definitely progress. "You've only got four weeks left. You might get desperate and tell someone."

"I might get desperate." He went for broke. Keeping a tight hold on her hand, he stepped in real close and ran a thumb over her cheek. Her eyes fluttered and, ever so slightly, she leaned into his hand. "But not *that* kind of desperate."

She let him kiss her, let him entwine his fingers with hers, let him pull her into his chest close enough that he could feel her nipples harden under her shirt. He'd give anything to get her out of that shirt so he could see those nipples for himself. God help him, her body was saying yes to a date and maybe a whole lot more. He had no idea what her mouth would say, though, so he hung back. Just a simple kiss, that's all.

If only the rest of their situation could be this simple.

A horn blared behind them, nearly sending them both out of their shoes. "Hey, buddy, you call for a tow?" the driver sneered out the window.

"Think about the date," he whispered to her as he let go of her hand.

"Okay."

Eight

A girl could tell a lot about a man by his vehicle. And according to the license plate, this seemed to be Dan's actual truck, not some rental. He'd driven all the way up from Texas.

Rosebud ran her hands over the premium leather of the passenger seat, trying to snoop without it looking like she was snooping. Dan had given her his keys after the tow-truck driver had called her "honey." It felt weird to just let a man take over for her, but frankly, she'd rather sit in the truck and try to figure out Dan Armstrong than stand next to that driver and wish she had some mace.

Dan had satellite radio. Of course he did. A man like Dan wouldn't want to listen to stations with commercial interruptions. She flipped through his preprogrammed channels. Willie's Place, Outlaw Country—those she expected. Dan probably hired those famous country singers to perform at company picnics or something ludicrous like that. But what came next surprised her—Alt Nation? Lithium? A Phish song filled the cab. She blinked hard in the dim light, but the name on the receiver stayed the same. Unreal. Not the standard cowboy tunes.

She went back on the dial until she found a Miranda Lambert song, then she looked around. The truck's interior was spotless—no crumpled-up wrappers or crushed cans underfoot, not even a layer of dust on the burled walnut dash. A shotgun hung on a rack on the rear window, but a quick look told her it either wasn't loaded or only had one round in the chamber. Did he always have that gun there, or was it just because of her "little" misfire?

She looked again. Man, it was a piece of work. The walnut stock was polished to a warm gleam, and the silver was inlaid with hunting dogs done in what looked like gold. The trigger looked like real gold, too. She didn't know much about high-end weapons, but she was willing to bet she could buy a house with the money that gun cost.

She began to feel a little out of place. Okay, a lot out of place. She'd caught glimpses of this kind of wealth during law school in D.C., but not even her boyfriend James had been this casually comfortable with the finest that money could buy. She was one step above dirt-poor. What the heck did an oil tycoon—because she was starting to realize that's what Dan was—want with the likes of her?

She was getting antsy. What was taking so long? She searched for Dan and the tow-truck driver in the rearview mirror. Dang. Dan had a heck of a rear view, all right. He was bent over the front end of her car, looking at the engine. Dan was doing a lot of pointing and the driver was doing a lot of head shaking. She didn't take all the gesturing as a positive development, which made the pit in her stomach grow a little wider. She had no idea if the hunk of steel was worth fixing, but it was the only car she had—and there was no way in hell she could afford a new one.

Lord, this seemed like a bad idea. Letting him pay for her

tow—and then letting him take her to dinner? On a date? Was Dan one of those guys who thought that dinner and car repairs guaranteed getting lucky?

She shuddered. She knew he was charming, handsome and under orders to trap her. But even given all that, she still couldn't help but feel—not think, but really and truly *feel*— that he was being totally up front with her. She thought back to their phone conversation. He hadn't said her name, or anything that would point to her. *He* wanted to ask *her* out.

She wanted to go out with *him*. If only his last name wasn't Armstrong.

Oh, what a mess she'd gotten herself into.

Well, she knew how to test his mettle. She dug out her notes as he got back in the cab.

"He's going to give you a call when it's ready." He set his hat on the dash and cocked his head to one side, listening to the song "Gunpowder and Lead." "You tryin' to tell me something?" he said with a grin as he fired up the truck.

The engine purred. A slight twinge of jealousy, so small she barely noticed it at all, flittered across Rosebud's mind. Wouldn't it be lovely to have a car that just *started* whenever she wanted it to? "Purely coincidental. And I'm also not a crazy ex-girlfriend."

Dan gave her a long look—long enough that Rosebud suddenly felt like she was on the witness stand. "I never did figure you for one." Then he shot her that confident smile again and began backing up. "I'll bring you back down, if you want, but it's going to be a few weeks."

"You really don't have to do that, but I appreciate it." A few weeks was a long time to be carless, but as long as she didn't have to leave the rez, she could ride her paint, Scout.

He shot her a snarky look out of the corner of his eye. "Besides, that'll give you the chance to do some more research. Where to?"

Would a date be such a bad thing? Two consenting adults having dinner and maybe another kiss? She had one left—and heaven help her, she hoped it was a good one. She scrambled to think of a place where Dan would be comfortable, but she was coming up blank. She'd hardly been able to afford fine dining when she'd gone to school here, and that had been almost seven years ago.

"Doesn't have to be anywhere fancy," Dan said, doing a pretty good job of interpreting her silence. "Anyplace with steak is fine by me."

She remembered Tanner had mentioned Bob's Roadhouse—he and Tom Yellow Bird used to hang out there back in the day. It must have been good—they'd gone back several times. "I know a place that's supposed to be good. Take a left here and head for the highway. And actually, I think I found everything I needed this time."

"Yeah? Digging up dirt on Cecil?"

"Nope." He didn't see this coming? She couldn't help but enjoy springing this on him. "You."

The truck lurched to a stop at an intersection. Even better than the wobbly chair, she decided. "Me?"

"You. This was the first chance I've had." The question was, would he own up to any of the stuff she'd found? Or was it all part of that undefined gray area? "You've got quite a public record, you know."

He sighed in resignation, slouching against his window. "You found the poster, didn't you?"

"This poster?" She slid the grainy grayscale poster out of the folder. The crummy printer had made it all but impossible to see what had been as plain as day on the computer screen—a young boy with a head full of blondish curls smiling up at an oil derrick. "You were literally the face of Armstrong Oil?"

"Cut me some slack. I was seven, and Dad bought me

ice cream for smiling." His fingers drummed on the steering wheel. "Mint chocolate chip, if I remember correctly. That damn poster floated around for almost ten years. I think every girl I went to high school with had a copy in her locker." He glanced over at her, the embarrassment making him look even more like the little boy in the picture. "*Not* worth the ice cream."

"*Cute* wasn't what you were going for in high school?"

He was in serious danger of pouting. But instead of looking childish, it illustrated what *cute* would look like on the man. "I hated it. That's why I did all the un-cute stuff."

"I'll give you *un-cute* for being on the honor roll for four years, but the rodeo team?" She clucked at him. Rodeo might not be cute, but she had a feeling that hadn't mattered to high-school girls. "No football?"

"Mom wouldn't let me play football. She was too worried about me getting hurt."

"Rodeo was safer than football? Now I've heard everything." The stats from the county fairs had been quite impressive. Dan made the time on broncos, won the steer wrestling and was unbeatable in calf roping. At least he'd earned that buckle the hard way. "Why didn't you go pro?"

"I said it was safer. Not safe. Mom rode barrels," he added by way of explanation. "Besides, didn't you ever do something a little wild, a little crazy?" His head swiveled to look her full in the eye.

"Does this count?" she asked, gesturing to the truck.

"Not yet, it doesn't." Even in the dim light of a summer night, she could still see the twinkle in his eye. "Why did you come all the way down here just to dig up that stuff? I would have told you if you'd asked."

That was the sort of statement that was easy to say after the fact. "Yeah?" She flipped to the more interesting stuff—the mug shot. "Tell me about college, then."

"Man," he groaned. "Remind me to avoid you in a court-room."

"Don't think of it as the Red Creek tribe asking about why you got arrested your sophomore year." She scooted around in her seat and tucked one leg under the other. "I'm asking. Just me."

"We haven't even had a date yet, and you want to know about that? That's third date stuff, at least."

"Maybe this is a date."

He glanced at her, a wide smile on his face. "Yeah?"

She had no right to feel so giddy about the smile he was wearing, but she couldn't help it. "*Maybe.* Now spill it. Destruction of college property? That doesn't seem like you, Dan."

He sighed again, but it seemed heavier this time. "When you went to college, what did you do?"

Not a good sign, if he was going to start turning the tables on her this early in the "date." "Well, I studied—"

"No, I mean, what did you *do?* Because when I went to college, I was tired of being Lewis Armstrong's boy, tired of eating steak, tired of being the poster boy for an oil company." He shook his head at the memory. "I missed my dad, but I didn't want to have to live up to him anymore."

Suddenly, this seemed like it was about a lot more than a drunken prank. "Like how?"

"You've heard of the metaphorical preacher's daughter?"

"Sure. The more religious the preacher, the more rebellious the daughter."

"I'm the son of a cattle-raising, oil-drilling, shotgun-owning, good old boy."

So that's why his hair had been past his shoulders and he'd been wearing those round glasses like John Lennon always wore. "You were a hippie?"

She liked him embarrassed—it was both cute and a little

bit sexy at the same time. "I tried. Did you know vegetarians don't eat *any* steak?"

"Shocking," she said in mock surprise. That explained the alternative channels. "How long did you last?"

"Almost two years at school, but the moment I came home, I was dying for a good hamburger." He chuckled at the memory. "I tried it all out. Smoked a little weed, burned a little incense, carried a few protest signs."

Normal hippies weren't known for their destructive tendencies. However…she put two and two together. "Hung out with a few ecoterrorists?"

"Proto-ecoterrorists," he corrected. "I made friends with some people."

"I've noticed you make friends with everyone."

"Not everyone," he corrected her with more force than she expected. He didn't like *someone,* that much was clear. "But most any reasonable person. That one time was the first and last time I ever did anything I truly regretted."

Despite the deep confession going on, Rosebud couldn't help but think that he didn't regret kissing her—either time. Her giddiness level rose. "What happened?"

He rubbed his seven-o'clock shadow. "When campus security showed up, I was the one holdin' the matches in front of a burning Dumpster. Oddly enough, no one believed that I was just trying to draw attention to the amount of garbage the school produced."

"You burned Dumpsters?" That wasn't *proto*-ecoterrorist in her book. "What did your mother do?"

"Well, first she cried, then she threatened to let the judge lock me up and throw away the key before I dragged my father's good name into the mud, then she cried some more." He shrugged in that embarrassed way again. "If I recall correctly, there was a lot of crying."

"I think I like your mother."

He chuckled, like maybe he agreed with her. "Between all the cryin' and the community service—I scrubbed a lot of garbage cans—I saw the light. A man doesn't like to upset his mama, you know."

"Not a good one, anyway." He shot an appreciative look at her.

This whole conversation had an air of the unreal to it. Rosebud should be holding on to this info, saving it for when she needed the leverage against Dan during negotiations, but instead, they were *just* talking. "So?"

"So, I grew up and joined the family business. Some of my old friends grew up and joined ELF."

She flipped through her notes. "The same ELF that targeted seven Armstrong Holdings derricks?"

"The very same. After the second time, when the police were still coming up empty, I started doing a little digging and all the signs pointed to my old buddies." He shook his head. "They knew it was my company—just punishing a traitor, I guess. I busted them red-handed one night. Oil derricks are a long way from Dumpsters, but they couldn't argue with a shotgun. They chose to negotiate instead of the alternative."

"Duly noted." She couldn't tell if that meant he had been willing to shoot, or if he'd have just turned them in to the authorities. She shivered. Her mind flashed back to that day in the valley—she'd never been sure if he'd had a gun on him or not. The *what-if* loomed *huge* in her mind. "So what was the truce? Take this exit, by the way."

He was silent as he took the exit that led to Bob's Roadhouse Bar and Grill. A bright red neon T-bone blinked above the sign advertising Rapid City Rollers Live Tonite. A line of motorcycles took up half the parking lot in front of a long, low building that looked like it was slouching to the left; a line of trucks filled the other half. Two people she hoped were only kissing backed up against a pickup truck, and another group was standing in a circle. Were they cheering? A flash of movement caught her eye, and she realized that a fight was going on in the middle. She shuddered.

Suddenly, Rosebud remembered why she'd never been here before. It was one thing for Tanner and Tom to go into a place like this—rough and gritty and full of people who were happy to throw a punch or three, all in the name of a good time. Tanner had always liked a game of pool and a loud band, and Tom—well, he'd never been afraid of anything, including what might happen to a couple of Lakota Indians in a white man's bar. The two of them wouldn't have had any trouble attracting plenty of feminine attention—or holding their own during the inevitable fights. Because the fights *were* inevitable.

She hated the way Tanner would come home with his face a bloody mess, telling her all about how he and Tom had shown those "racist *wasicu*," those white devils, what a true Lakota warrior could do. Tanner may have lived clean and sober, but he had still itched for the fight and lived to count coup on his enemy.

As if his face wasn't warning enough, Tanner had always lectured her on staying away from places like Bob's. *"Promise me,"* he'd say, his eyes serious as she patched up his cuts. *"Promise me you won't go to a place like that. It's too dangerous for you."*

He'd made her so mad back then. Always trying to tell her what she could and could not do. He'd been the one who'd sent all the cute boys packing because no one was good enough for his sister. He had been the one who'd told her she had to go to law school. And every time he told her to make that promise, she'd wanted to strangle him. *"Oh, you're the only one allowed to do stupid things?"*

But every time, Tanner would only shake his head. *"Just promise, little sister."*

At the time, she hadn't thought Tanner would ever run into something that was too dangerous for him. She'd always thought he'd be able to take whatever came his way. Until that night… *"Promise."*

The neon sign seemed less bright, and more like blood spilling into the night. This place was dangerous. The promise was old and Tanner was dead, but that didn't change what she'd promised.

She looked over at Dan, the words *Let's go somewhere else* right on her lips.

But then she saw the look on his face—a broad smile, fingers tapping on the steering wheel. "Now this is my kind of joint!" he said, checking out the row of bikes.

"Are you sure you don't want something else? Something nicer?"

He only shook his head. "There's a lot to be said for a good old-fashioned honky-tonk on a Saturday night." He turned a blinding smile to her. "Almost feels like home."

Shoot. Well, she'd gotten herself into this mess. Unless she wanted to admit—out loud—that she was scared *and* had no clue about dining options of any sort, she had no choice but to tough it out. And if she stayed close to Dan, no one would give her any trouble, right?

Swallowing down her hesitation, she turned to Dan. It took a second for her to remember what they had been talking about. Oh, yeah. Ecoterrorists staring down the business end of a shotgun. "So, about that truce?" She'd just focus on Dan—which was also dangerous, but in a totally different way.

"Bribery," he said as he unbuckled his seat belt. "Once, they were my friends. I couldn't forget that. So certain people who shall remain nameless are on the company payroll."

Not what she'd expected. "Seriously? That's the truce?"

"That and the fact that if anything else happens to my

pumps, the FBI will be all over them like white on rice. I'm literally the only outsider to know who some of these people are."

She was silent for a moment. He really could keep a secret—did that include car repairs and dates? "Is that what this is? A bribe? My car magically gets fixed and I'm supposed to shut up and go away?"

His hand was on the door, seconds from opening it, but he froze. Moving at glacier speed, he turned, his face hard to read in the flashing red light. And then his thumb brushed against her cheek before he wrapped his hand around the back of her neck, pulling her to him until their foreheads were touching. She flinched. He was going to kiss her—the third kiss. Three and she was out.

"I don't want you to shut up," he said in a whisper that made his drawl sound like it belonged in a bedroom. "And I most definitely do not want you to go away, darlin'." His other hand traced the hollow in her neck before it drifted down to her shoulders, leaving a trail of fire in its wake.

But he didn't kiss her. He didn't even cop a feel. She wasn't out yet.

"What *do* you want, Dan?" Her heart pounded away in her chest as her hands found their way to his cheeks. The stubble scratched at her palms, small pricks of irritation that did nothing but turn her on. Kind of like Dan himself. *Tell me the truth,* she thought. *A truth I can believe.*

"I want to buy you dinner, and if the band is halfway decent, I want to dance you around."

"Is that all?"

"Nope." He touched his lips to her forehead, leaving a scorch mark on her skin. Not a kiss, she quickly justified. Didn't count if it wasn't on the lips, which conveniently meant she wasn't out yet. *Anything* to still be in—even Bob's Roadhouse Bar and Grill. "But that's all I'm asking for right now."

Nine

His "please" smile got them a quiet table in the back of the restaurant—quiet, that is, by bar standards. They only had to shout a little over something that sounded like Charlie Daniels locked in a closet with KISS and an angry cat. "Halfway decent" was pushing it, but the dance floor was packed with every shade of hick, good old boy and white trash possible. The Rapid City Rollers were apparently quite a draw, Dan mused as they looked over the menus. He hadn't been honky-tonkin' for a good long time, and not with a pretty lady by his side for even longer. He was glad she'd picked this place. He wanted to show her that he wasn't all thousand-dollar hats and million-dollar oil wells—he was perfectly happy being a regular guy, if that's what she wanted to see. The night was shaping up real nice.

"Four-drink minimum," a skinny waitress with unreal blond hair yelled as she bounced her pen on the pad. She pointed her chin toward a handwritten sign over the bar. "4 Drinks, No Execptions. $4 Longnecks Friday and Saterday," it announced. *Exceptions* and *Saturday* were misspelled. "What'll ya'll have?"

"Bud—in the bottle—and the T-bone, bloody," Dan shouted back. Then he looked at Rosebud.

Her sweet mouth was twisted off to one side. She looked like she was five seconds from wrapping all her hair back up in a business braid and grilling him under oath. Great. Now what had he done? "I'll have the New York strip, medium, and a Coke."

"Four-drink minimum," the waitress repeated, slamming the tip of the pen for each drawn-out word, like she was talking to a little kid. "Four, understand?"

"I can count," Rosebud shot back, slapping her menu on the table.

Both women bristled, and Dan had that weird out-of-time feeling again, like he'd waltzed into a saloon in 1886 instead of into a bar in the twenty-first century. What next—armed bandits holding up a stagecoach? "We're here for the band," he said with his best smile as he dug out two twenties and a ten and placed them on top of the menus he handed back to the waitress. Pre-tipping never hurt anyone. "Four drinks shouldn't be a problem."

He couldn't hear over the wailing music, but he thought Rosebud hissed. For her part, the waitress broke into an ugly grin and winked at Dan. "No, I guess not. Two steaks, coming right up, *sugar*." So much for the night being real nice. This was starting to look like a bad idea.

This time, Rosebud definitely hissed. He looked at her. She was hunched defensively, her eyes darting around the room. Anything good he'd started in the truck was long gone. "I take it you've never been in here," Dan said, hoping to keep the conversation as light as possible while still screaming over the music.

She shot him a smile that looked ferocious, but Dan

watched as she got herself back under control. Her mouth untwisted as she leaned back in her chair, one arm slung over the back. At least she was trying. "No, I've never attempted this before." The way she said it made it clear that she ranked honky-tonking right up there with skydiving without a parachute.

If she'd never been here, why had she picked this place? There had to be other restaurants in this town. But rather than put her on the spot, he tried to keep things positive. "There's a first for everything, huh?"

For a second, Dan wished they were back in the truck. Not that he loved getting grilled about his past, but Rosebud was way too on edge in this place, and he had no idea why.

He glanced around. Seemed like a run-of-the-mill honky-tonk to him. On second glance, he noticed everyone was looking at her, and not like he looked at her. No, just about every female in the joint was glaring at Rosebud out the corner of their eyes like she was wearing a huge scarlet *A*—and no pants. Most of the men had taken notice, too, but Dan decided he didn't like those looks anymore.

Dan couldn't figure out where the attitude came from until it hit him like a bolt out of the blue. Rosebud was the only Indian in a sea of white faces. Over the din of the band, he remembered that weasel Naylor sputtering out *savages* and the way his uncle talked down to that slime Thrasher. No doubt about it, Dan thought as he mentally smacked his head. This attempt at a date *was* a bad idea.

They should go. Dan started to stand, but he caught the defiant way Rosebud crossed her arms and lifted her chin. She may not be comfortable here, but she showed no sign of bolting. Of course she wouldn't. She wouldn't turn tail when Cecil wanted her gone, and she wouldn't bail now. Somehow, he knew she would never give anyone the satisfaction of defeating her.

He settled back into his chair, positioning himself between her and the crowd. If she wasn't about to run and hide, he wasn't, either.

The waitress flitted past, setting down their drinks. Dan caught the way Rosebud stared at his beer. "Is this okay?" he asked, taking a cautious swig.

She shrugged and scooted her chair next to his. It was only natural to put his arm around her shoulders and make sure she knew she was safe with him.

"How much do you know about me, Dan?" The way she leaned up to speak in his ear, using a nearly normal tone, was more than enough to make him forget about all the dirty looks they were getting.

"I've done my research." A little bit of the internet went a long way.

"So you know about my parents?"

Parents? Who the hell wanted to talk about parents at a time like this? But she was resting her head on his shoulder. She fit there real nice. He sighed and dredged through his memory. "They died in a car wreck, didn't they?"

"Dad was drunk—they both were. Drove into a tree. The official report blames the road conditions, but I know what really happened."

Midswig, Dan paused. "Tanner didn't drink." He remembered now—that was one of Rosebud's main arguments against the suicide ruling. Tanner Donnelly didn't drink; therefore, he couldn't have been drunk enough to shoot his head off.

She sighed, a sound of sheer weariness. "No."

"You don't drink."

"No."

He swallowed and nearly choked on his beer. Suddenly, that four-drink minimum looked like a mountain because, as much as he wanted a few beers, having more than one and then climbing behind the wheel wasn't an option. "I'll just have the one, and we won't leave until I'm stone-cold sober, okay?"

"But the waitress—"

Speak of the devil. The waitress leaned over his shoulder, grazing him with her boobs. "Get you another one, sugar?"

Next time he managed to talk Rosebud into anything resembling a date, it was going to be someplace quiet and secluded. He'd thought the tribal members had given him the cold shoulder at that first meeting—but if this was how they were treated by white folks off the reservation, he couldn't blame them.

Rosebud had never treated him coldly, though—all of her chill seemed to be an occupational hazard. When she wasn't being a lawyer, she looked at him with a gaze that was much warmer. Although he had no idea if he was going to get any warmth in this bar. He sighed in frustration. What they needed was some neutral territory. "You know, I'd like to buy the band a round." He dug out two more twenties. "That's…" he leaned forward and counted. "Four beers. Keep the change." If that's what it cost to buy them a little breathing room in this place, then that's what it cost.

The waitress snatched the bills out of his hand and shoved one into her back pocket. "Anything you want, sugar."

"If she calls you that again, I'm going to rip her lips off," Rosebud whispered as the waitress finally left them alone. She sounded serious, too.

The note of jealousy had him grinning. "I wouldn't want you to get your hands dirty."

"Do you do this often? Go out to the dives and pay too much for beer?"

"Naw." He leaned in—so she could hear him better, not so he could catch a hint of her scent. "And before you ask, I don't spend all my time in an exclusive club sipping martinis, either. I don't have the time for that, and I don't often have anyone I want to go out with, either."

Rosebud took a long sip of her Coke before she settled back into his arm. "What about Tiffany?"

What was he going to do with—to—this woman? "I suppose I should have seen that one coming."

"Probably," she agreed. He couldn't see her face, but her shoulders sort of moved, like she was giggling at him.

"If I tell you about Tiffany, will you be done researching me?"

Unexpectedly, her hand wrapped around his waist and she hooked a finger through a belt loop as she molded herself to his chest. The full-body contact—oh, sweet Jesus, the weight of her breasts pressed against him—made his erection try to stand up and salute. "Well, done with the secondhand research, anyway."

Which left firsthand possibilities wide-open. He shifted his hips until he was certain that the table was covering them both from the waist down. "Deal. What do you want to know?" Talking about his oldest lady friend didn't seem like foreplay, but if it worked for Rosebud, then it worked for him.

"I counted about thirty or so mentions of you two in the society pages of the Dallas papers—none of which involved places like this. That seems like a lot for not having anyone you want to go out with."

He knew what this was. This was Rosebud trying to figure out if he was a love-'em-and-leave-'em kind of guy or not. Full disclosure was the only way to go. "Tiffany's a wonderful girl. I haven't seen her since I danced with her at her wedding, though. She thought that was for the best. She still sends me Christmas cards. Got a couple of cute babies now. Her husband's a real nice fellow."

"Why didn't you marry her?"

He went stiff, and not in the fun way. Just when he thought he'd gone and figured this woman out, she went and asked him something like that. Hands down, this was the weirdest date he'd ever been on. "I didn't want a wife."

She stilled against him. "What *do* you want, Dan?"

That was the second time she'd asked him that question tonight. If they were going to get all deep, he sure wished he could have another beer. "Tiffany was what I needed in Texas—someone to go to charity balls with, someone who understood that my company comes first."

"Men have married for less than that."

"I don't want a wife," he repeated with more force. "I want a partner. I don't want someone to cook my dinner and make my bed. I don't want a maid. I want an equal. I want someone I can talk to, someone I can respect."

Someone like Rosebud.

The thought popped into his head like a prairie dog popping out of the ground.

Dan had thought once—only once—about actually marrying Tiffany, but aside from the sex and the next corporate dinner party, he didn't actually have a single interesting thing to say to her, and vice versa.

Despite his little outburst, he realized he was stroking her hair. And that she was still holding on to him. She didn't say anything, but she hadn't run screaming, either.

The waitress shot Rosebud a look when she came back with the steaks, but when Dan pleased and thanked her for a Coke to go with his meal, he got the kind of smile a waitress gives a big tipper. Man, he'd forgotten how hungry he was, and the steak was bleeding red. Perfect.

"What about you?" he said between bites of meat.

She was digging in herself, which he found refreshing. Too many times he'd taken a woman out to dinner only to have her pick at a sad little salad. "What do you want to know?"

Well, now, that was a change of pace. "I found some stuff. I'm honored to be in the presence of the Indian Days Powwow Princess."

She rolled her eyes, but still gave him a royal wave. "I bet there was a picture with that one."

"Yup." In fact, she'd looked exactly like an old-fashioned Indian princess—her hair in two tight braids, her dress covered with those little jingly cone things—but not a whole lot like *his* Indian princess, the one in the simple buckskin dress with loose hair. Except for the smile—Rosebud's smile of victory. "But there were huge holes." In fact, all he'd found were the honor rolls. Top of her high school class, summa cum laude all four years at the university, top twenty-five percent in law school. That, and the ongoing legal battle with Armstrong Holdings. That was it.

She grinned at him, fork hovering in the air. "Some of us have the good sense to stay out of the society pages."

"Trust me, I'm all for keeping a low profile these days."

Her eyes shot over his shoulder. He followed her gaze and saw their waitress standing with several other barmaids, doing everything but pointing. "You need more practice." At least she sounded amused. He hoped.

"Tell me about the holes. Do you like being a lawyer?"

Her face hardened a little, but not so much that she stopped chewing. "I'm good at it."

"Now, ain't that jest like a lawyer," he said in his heaviest drawl. "Answerin' the question she wants to answer, not the question I *asked*."

She notched an eyebrow at him that said, *Oh, come on.* "Well, I am. But I wanted to study art—fiber arts. I..." Her eyes dipped down, and he swore she was blushing. "I like to quilt."

Quilting? At first, that surprised him, but then he thought

about it. One tiny stitch at a time, over and over, until the big picture was finished. Methodical. "I bet you're good at it."

Even in the dim light of the bar, the blush deepened. Now he was getting somewhere. "I don't get the chance to do it very much. Something *else* takes up all my time."

"I don't want to talk about *that*," he said, finishing his beer. No way was Cecil invited to any part of this party.

"Agreed." He watched her finish her steak fries. She caught him looking. "What?"

"I'm just curious."

She sort of smiled, in that grimacing kind of way. "About?"

"What else you did while you were staying out of the society pages."

"That's not a proper question."

"Technicalities. You know all about Tiffany. Did you ever have a boyfriend?"

"Ever?" She snorted at him, but at the same time, she pushed her plate away and leaned back into him. "You make it sound like I'm either a nun or a leper."

"You're a beautiful woman," he replied, settling his arm back around her. It just felt so easy, so right. "I bet you've had a lot of men chasing you."

"You have no idea."

"Why don't you give me one?"

She giggled—yeah, he was sure that's what the gentle shaking meant. "I worked at a coffee bar to help pay for college. It didn't take long to figure out that more lipstick meant better tips."

"That's just guys hitting on you—most any red-blooded American male would do that. That's not what I'm askin' about."

Her hand looped back around his waist. Maybe she felt

safer there—or maybe she liked it. Either way, he wasn't about to shoo her away. "I had one, once. In law school."

"A boyfriend?"

"Was Tiffany your girlfriend?"

"Not really. She was just…convenient." Which sounded bad, but happened to be the truth. Convenient for both of them, really, until it wasn't anymore. That's when it had ended with a smile and a handshake.

"Friends with benefits," she agreed. "That's what James was."

Lucky bastard. The name rang a faint bell, but he couldn't place it. Dan could only hope this James had known how lucky he was. "A James doesn't sound like your type."

"He wasn't. He was from this real blue blood D.C. family." She sighed. Her free hand was resting on his thigh now, and he thought she might be swaying to the beat of the music a little. Dancing was about to occur. Whether or not they made it to the dance floor remained to be seen. "No one knew. He wouldn't have ever taken me home to meet his parents, and there was no way in hell he would have made it one day on the rez. Just one of those things."

He pulled her to her feet and led her out onto the dance floor. Whatever this thing between them was, it would be different from what she'd had with James, from what he'd had with Tiffany, he decided as the band began to butcher some Toby Keith song. Because Rosebud was different.

With one hand on her waist, the other wrapped around her fingers, he led her into the crowd of two-steppers. Space was tight, so he was forced to hold her real close as they moved in small circles around the floor.

His mouth found her ear. It took just about everything he had not to wrap his tongue around her earlobe. "What about this?"

"This what?" She tilted her head into his until they were

dancing cheek-to-cheek, which sure as hell seemed like an invitation to him.

"Is this 'just one of those things'?" He actually felt a little nervous about the question, mostly because he had no idea what she'd say.

She didn't answer for a few beats, but then she pulled away, just far enough that she could look him in the eyes. "No," she said, and her soft voice found his ears despite the thumping bass beat. "This isn't."

She kissed him. *She* kissed *him,* and not one of those slow-building, wait-and-see kisses like the ones he'd been giving her. She bit his lower lip as her fingers dug into his shoulder. *She's hungry,* he thought as she devoured his mouth.

He went hard in a second. Given that there was no space between them, she knew it immediately, and answered by grinding her hips into his. She was going to bring him to his knees, right in the middle of the dance floor. He fought back the only way he could, by kissing her with a vengeance. Yeah, they were supposed to be two-stepping around the floor, but he pulled her hand in close enough to their bodies that he was able to graze her breast with his thumb. She shuddered into him with a moan he felt more than heard.

They had to get out of here, pronto.

Finally, she saved him from himself by pulling back, just enough that he could catch his breath. "Three," she breathed, her eyes closed as she licked her lips at a painfully slow speed.

"Three?" His brain wasn't working, but he wasn't sure he cared, just so long as she kept kissing him like that. "You wanna get out of here?"

Starving, he thought as she looked at him, the need in her eyes naked for the world to see. "Yeah. Let's go."

The bar was more crowded and the band was louder, but finally they made it back to their table, hands locked together. "Just give me a second," she said, pointing at the rest-rooms sign.

"Okay." Hell, she could have a whole minute if she wanted, as long as they got out of here and went...where?

Damn, he thought as she disappeared down the hall. They probably couldn't go back to her place, and Cecil's house was out of the question. Once they'd left the university area, he didn't remember seeing a single hotel that had a room for the night, and, damn it all, he didn't want to make love to her in the front seat of his truck. He may be hard up, but that was crass. She deserved silk sheets and whirlpool tubs big enough for two.

Neutral territory. For some reason, the blueprints he'd been looking at this afternoon—a lifetime ago, it seemed—popped into his mind. No, not the blueprints. The map of Armstrong land and the Dakota River underneath them.

A small building, he remembered seeing now. Just a dinky square next to a little creek that fed into the Dakota, about seven miles from the dam site and a long way away from anything else. No roads went there, no power lines, either. At the time, he hadn't thought much of it, but now, in his desperation, he wondered what that building was. If it was a cabin, territory didn't get much more neutral than that. Probably didn't have silk sheets or room service, but if it was quiet...

They couldn't get there tonight. But this wasn't just about tonight. This was about—

"Hey!" A shrill shout broke above the ending chord of a song. "I said— Dan! *Help!*"

Ten

Rosebud pushed her way down the crowded hall to the ladies' room, her head swimming. Someone shoved her, but she barely noticed. Three kisses, and she was *supposed* to be out, but she was in deeper than she'd ever thought possible. They were leaving and she didn't know where they were going, but she'd officially stopped caring the moment he'd touched her. That clear moment of sheer heat made thinking an unnecessary, unwelcome action. Instead, the only action she wanted was to peel his jeans right off him and see exactly what she'd been missing.

Three kisses, three years. How could she have forgotten what she was missing? Maybe it was because James had never made her feel quite this hot, and certainly never this weak. Unlike the other white men she'd known before college, James had never treated her like The Indian, which had been a relief. But he'd never really treated her like a lover, either. She'd just been a girl he knew, just as he'd always been a boy she knew. Just some guy she occasionally went to bed with.

To Dan, she was a woman, pure and simple. Not merely a lawyer or an Indian, but all of those things and more. In his arms, she felt alive. To hell with dams and lawsuits, family members long gone and still here. Right now, she was really living.

Which was why she chose to ignore all the drunk and disorderly people around her. It didn't matter how evil their glances were. The only eyes she was concerned with were Dan's.

She pushed her way into the ladies' room. The bathroom wasn't big, but it was packed. The air was thick with hairspray, cheap perfume and industrial-strength air freshener as women crowded around each sink and mirror, a sea of bottled blond, exposed bra straps and short skirts.

By the time the door shut behind her, the whole bathroom had come to a silent halt. Mascara wands froze in midair, cigarettes dangled from lipsticked mouths and every eye was on her.

Damn. Her euphoric high dissipated in a heartbeat. That waitress was in the corner, giving Rosebud a look she'd seen before, too many times to count.

She'd seen it the first day of junior high, when her aunt had arranged for Rosebud to go to a successful white school off the rez. She still remembered the way the girls had acted like she was a blatant threat. No one had talked to her for months, but the rumors had reached her ears anyway. She stole purses, did drugs, screwed the teachers, ate garbage, had the IQ of a dog and on and on.

What was she to do then? She'd only been twelve. She wasn't the fighter Tanner had been, so she did what Aunt Emily told her. She said nothing. She looked at no one. She'd done the best work she could do. The first time she'd said something in social studies—in February—the teacher was shocked that Rosebud actually knew how to speak English.

After that, Rosebud had found her own way. She didn't brawl like Tanner, but she refused to be silent. The next time she'd heard the whispers, she went on the offensive. Her mouth was her gift, so she used it. But that was then, in the relative safety of a public school. The worst that had happened was the fat lip she'd gotten for pointing out that one of her tormenters wasn't smart enough to know that her boyfriend was cheating on her with her so-called best friend.

This was now, in the middle of a dive bar in a state with concealed carry laws on the books. She was not welcome. She swallowed, torn between a flash of panic and her always intense need to be in control of the situation. Control? Please. This was fast becoming one of the more dangerous situations she'd been in.

No fear, she decided as she strode to the only open stall, her head up and her shoulders back.

Just as she sat down, the stall door shuddered under the weight of a sudden, silent kick, quickly followed by a second. Rosebud managed not to scream, but she clutched her purse to her chest. The third hit was higher, like someone using the palm of her hand, but the fourth one was another kick. Rosebud braced a leg against the door as it bowed, and each succeeding kick felt like a sledgehammer driving into her hip socket.

Peeing while every single woman smacked or kicked the door on their way out was nothing if not challenging, but finally, the room was silent. Rosebud managed to finish. Before she opened the stall door, she listened, but she couldn't hear the sound of breathing over the reverberations of the band.

Just to be sure, she dug in her purse until she came up with a ballpoint pen. Her gun would have been better, but guns and university libraries didn't mix. A ballpoint would have to do.

She slung her sack over her shoulder and slowly opened the door. Empty, thank God. Even that waitress was gone. Rosebud washed quickly, reviewing her exit strategy. She had twenty-five feet of hallway to get through, and then another fifteen feet to get to Dan. She assumed he was still at their table, waiting for her. If she went low and fast, she might be able to snake through the crowd without anyone noticing her.

Hell, who was she kidding? Almost half the place knew she was in here.

I am not afraid, she thought, as if thinking it would make it so. Taking a few deep breaths, she clutched the pen like a knife. She'd stab anyone who tried to stop her. Sometimes, self-defense was the only defense. Forty feet. She could do it. She barreled out the door.

She only made the first twenty feet before she ran into a wall of bikers. Actually, it was just one biker, but he made a wall all by himself, completely blocking the last few feet of the hallway. "Well, now," the man said, leering down at her.

The overwhelming smell of onions and whiskey smacked her upside the face. She couldn't see past the do-rag embroidered with flames on his head—where the hell was Dan? Before she could sidestep him, he grabbed the arm that had the pen. "My buddy bet me twenty bucks I couldn't get you to dance with me, Pocahontas."

That was her least favorite racist nickname, the one that irritated her like lemon juice in a paper cut. She tried to twist out of his grip, but the jerk held tight as he pulled her toward the dance floor. At least they weren't in the hall anymore. Her eyes shot around the bar, but she didn't see Dan. Where the hell was he?

"Sorry," she said, forcing herself to smile while she tried to peel his fingers off her biceps. Why were bikers always so burly? "I'm afraid you're going to lose that bet."

"One dance, little squaw. I saw you out there dancing with that cowboy. I want some of that sugar."

Squaw. She took it back. *That* was her least favorite nickname. "Let me go," she said with more force, hoping she sounded serious instead of just terrified.

It didn't work. "You think you're too good for me? Is that it? You're just some damn Injun!" He hauled her up, closer to his face.

"Hey!" That did it. Screw this scared thing. She wasn't going down without a fight. She kicked toward his groin as hard as she could, ever thankful she'd worn her boots today. "I said—"

The biker snarled a curse at her. He didn't let go, but he did bend double. Confident that she'd connected with his nuts the first time, Rosebud tried for two.

Suddenly, her head whipped back with enough force that she lost her footing. Between the hold the biker had on her arm and whoever had a death grip on her hair, she was suddenly, completely helpless. Fight or no, she was going down. "Dan! *Help!*"

The biker staggered to his knees, pulling her down with him, but she couldn't go far. "You little slut," a female voice screeched behind her as her head jerked back again. Rosebud saw stars. "What did you do to my man?"

"Dan!" Rosebud screamed at the top of her lungs. Pain and fear were duking it out, and the fear was winning.

Her head jerked again. A sharp pain on her forehead blinded her to everything else. That waitress wouldn't scalp her, would she? "Savage," the woman's voice said, close to her ear, as calm and as clear as the noon sun. "I'll teach you to show your red face around here."

Oh, hell, she would. She *was*.

Rosebud heard bones crunch, but instead of feeling the searing pain that should have gone with it, she only heard the biker's howl.

"Let her go." Dan. Even better, he sounded furious—worse than when he'd realized she'd shot at him.

Her arm was free. In the next second, her head was free and she fell. But instead of hitting the floor, she fell into familiar arms and was up on her feet before she knew what was going on. Blinking the tears out of her eyes, she saw that Dan was standing on the biker's hand. He had one arm looped under both of hers to hold her up, and in the other he had a knife. A knife? Rosebud's eyes narrowed in on the flash of metal, but it still took a few seconds for her to realize it was a steak knife from dinner.

"She kicked my balls!" The biker wailed from the floor. Dan responded by grinding his heel in a little harder. "My hand!"

"I don't want any trouble," Dan said, his voice low—but she heard him loud and clear. He swung around, blade out, pulling Rosebud with him. The music, she realized. The band had stopped playing. The entire bar was silent. Off to her left, the unmistakable sound of a pump-action shotgun filled the air. "No trouble," he repeated.

They were going to die, all because Dan asked her out on a date and she'd had the nerve to say yes.

"Walk," Dan said under his breath. His hand was clamped around her ribs, so when he took a step forward, he practically carried her with him.

Rosebud was too afraid to look in the direction of the shotgun, too afraid to look at anyone but Dan in case they took that as an act of aggression. She kept her eyes focused on his hand and the blade. A steak knife was a hell of a lot better than a pen. He held it like he wasn't afraid to use it, but it still didn't beat a shotgun. She didn't want to die in this bar. The steak hadn't even been that good.

Dan spun around again, careful to make sure she followed. They were backing toward the door, she realized. Freedom.

"She started it!" That had to be the waitress, screeching at the top of her lungs.

Rosebud tensed, afraid that was the straw and she was about to become the camel's back. She couldn't even protest her innocence. Her throat was clogged with terror—if anything came out, it would be a scream.

"I don't care who started it. I'll finish it." How in the hell could Dan manage to sound so calm? They were outnumbered two hundred to two, and he sounded like he was negotiating a business deal!

Rosebud heard the sound of chairs scraping over the floor, but they kept moving backward. "Get ready," he whispered to her. A rush of night air hit her in the back of the neck, and then suddenly they were outside while all those angry faces were still inside. Dan let go of the knife and the tip stuck into a wood slat of the porch at the same time his fingers unglued themselves from her ribs. "The truck," he said. "Now!"

They ran so fast that Rosebud couldn't hear anything but her own sounds—her breathing, her heartbeat—so she couldn't tell if anyone was behind her. She sure as hell wasn't going to stop and check. Dan had a hold of her arm now, pulling her along with him in the mad dash to his truck. They made it in seconds. "Get down," he ordered as he cranked the engine.

"Your shotgun?" she asked. Adrenaline flooded her system. Part of her wanted to fire that bad boy off. They wanted a savage? By God, she'd give them savage.

"No," he replied, still pulling off calm even as the truck peeled out of the parking lot. He adjusted the mirror and zigged the truck left. "Just stay down for a minute. We're almost clear."

A huge boom exploded behind them, and Rosebud screamed as the truck lurched hard right. Dan floored it.

"They just fired over us," he said, like this whole assault was no big deal. "We're on the highway, darlin'. We're okay now."

Rosebud tried to nod, tried to do something, but the last ten minutes flashed through her mind again—the bathroom door shuddering, the guy's repulsive breath as he manhandled her, the way her neck snapped when her hair had been yanked. She touched her forehead and her fingers came away with a smear of blood. Her stomach rolled. "I'm going to be sick," she gasped.

"Hold on." The truck picked up speed, and then took another hard right before coming to a screeching halt.

She flung the door open and stumbled out of the truck, landing on her knees on a gravelly patch of scrub grass. Her stomach gave up the fight.

Suddenly, her hair was pulled up and away from her face, and a warm hand rubbed between her shoulder blades. Oh, just wonderful. Here she was, throwing up her guts and a bad steak in front of Dan. She supposed it beat the hell out of gunshot wounds, but at this exact moment in time, things couldn't get any worse. The sickening embarrassment brought on another round of heaving.

When she was finished, she sat back on her heels. Dan crouched down next to her, still holding her hair. "Better?"

"Um...um..." No. But even in her weakest moment, with the undeniable evidence all over the shoulder of the road, she couldn't admit it.

Dan's eyes searched her all over. She couldn't meet his gaze—she didn't know if she'd ever be able to again. "I'll right back."

Rosebud sat there in a state of shock, and all she could coherently think was, *You knew it was three and you were out, girl. And this is* out.

Dan's footsteps crunched on the gravel behind her, and then he held out a bottle of water and a damp cloth. She rinsed out her mouth, which helped tremendously. "Hold still," he said, and he wiped her face for her.

The cut stung, but the pain told her it was small. "It's not bad," he said, his voice doing its level best to be calm. He cupped her chin in his palm and tilted her head toward the truck's headlights.

Suddenly the terror that had been clogging her throat dissolved into hysterical cries. Clamping her eyes shut, she tried to bite them back.

"I'm sorry. It was all my fault."

This time, the tears wouldn't be bitten back, choked down or hidden until she was alone. "I'm going to cry now," she managed to say as the sobs broke free. "But I don't want this to negatively impact your opinion of me in the courtroom."

Dan gave her a look that made it quite clear Rosebud had officially lost it. "It won't."

"And this in no way reflects on our date—before the attack," she sobbed. She sounded hysterical. The fear and pain and relief all melted into one major circuit overload, one that apparently tripped several wires in her head, because suddenly she couldn't stop babbling. "It was a nice date. I actually like you a whole lot. If only your name wasn't Armstrong. If only you weren't *that* Armstrong, Dan."

The next thing she knew, the gravel wasn't digging into her knees anymore. Dan was clutching her to his chest and carrying her back to the truck, but he didn't set her down. Instead, he slid into the seat and held her on his lap, her feet dangling out the door. He rocked her back and forth as he stroked her hair and whispered, "I know, darlin'. I know," over and over, which Rosebud took as a sign that she was still talking.

She had no idea what she was saying.

Eleven

Slow and easy, Dan said to himself as he tried to walk calmly into the Red Creek tribal headquarters Monday morning.

So what if the last time he'd seen Rosebud had been at about three in the morning on Sunday? So what if she hadn't let him walk her to her door? So what if she hadn't returned either of his calls yesterday? So what if he was nigh on to frantic with worry about her? As far as he knew, no one else was aware of the busted car, the dinner date or the near scalping, and he wasn't about to give anything away by running around like some fool chicken with its head cut off.

"Good morning, Mr. Armstrong," Judy said, cup of coffee ever at the ready. "Ms. Donnelly is running a few minutes late. She'll be with you shortly."

He couldn't help it. He looked past Judy, past the conference room door, down the long hall. Somewhere down there, Rosebud had an office. He prayed she was in it. "But she's here, right?"

"Of course." Judy blocked the hall and motioned Dan to the depressing conference room.

Resigned to his fate, Dan handed over the cookie bars Maria had made and took to doing laps around the conference table. If Rosebud didn't get her behind in here in five minutes, he was going looking for her.

He was reaching for the doorknob when it turned and Judy appeared, carrying a different box of files. Behind her, Rosebud stood by the door, her eyes focused on something Dan couldn't see. It reminded Dan of that first day he'd come to the reservation, when Joe White Thunder had acted like Dan didn't exist. Bad sign. She had a small bandage over the cut, but she otherwise looked normal. Hair in that braid-bun thing, the suit over a light blue shirt, glasses settled firmly on her nose.

Rosebud stood stock-still until the receptionist was gone, and then she silently shut the door. Dan fought the urge to rush to her and pull her into his arms. He tried to tell himself that she was just upset, which was a far cry better than hysterical. Her behavior seemed like more than upset, though. She was acting like they were strangers.

Finally, he broke the tense silence. "Are you okay?"

"Fine." That was a lie. He could see her biting the inside of her lip. "I knocked my head against a kitchen cabinet."

"Oh. Of course." As good a story as any. "I was worried about you." He felt obliged to drop his voice down to a whisper. "I called. Twice."

She flinched, but finally, she looked *at* him, instead of *through* him. "My aunt was home."

"I'm really sorry," he blurted out, desperate to get some sort of reaction out of her. "I should have waited to take you to a better restaurant. I should have put that waitress in her place. I should have waited for you outside the bathroom."

Those were the top three things he'd done wrong, but he was hard-pressed to tell which one would have kept her safe.

She moved slowly, like she had a raging headache. "It wasn't your fault," she said as she settled into her chair. "I should have known better than to—"

"Wait—what happened Saturday night wasn't your fault."

"Of course it was," she continued, selecting a file from the top of the box and opening it up as if they were just reviewing the facts for the upcoming court date. She didn't even sound angry. "I..." Finally, Dan saw a crack in her professional demeanor. She closed her eyes and took a deep breath. "I appreciate your offer to pay me for my time, but that won't be necessary."

"What about your car?"

"Aunt Emily has a car I can use if I need to leave the reservation."

"So you're just going to stay on the rez for the rest of your life?"

"This is where I belong."

She was pissing him off, plain and simple. "You're going to let a bunch of dumb hicks at one bar scare you off like that? If you want, I'll buy the damn place and raze it to the ground."

Her hand smacked the table. The sudden pop made him jump. "You don't get it, do you? It's not just one bar. Believe it or not, that's just how people around here treat me. Us. Ignorant savages and slutty squaws—the only good Indian is a dead one."

Dan's jaw dropped. "That's not how I treat you, and you know it."

For a second, she looked away, but then she came right back at him, both barrels blazing. "No? Get back to me in three and a half weeks, Dan. Then we'll see how you treat me."

Damn his uncle. Dan had thought it before, lots of times,

but he'd never meant it as much as he did right now. Just as Rosebud had said that night, if only he wasn't that Armstrong—an Armstrong like Cecil. "I don't give a damn about that dam. That is *not* what this is about."

"Then what?"

He grabbed that crappy chair and pulled it up next to her so that he could look her in the eye. "This is about you and me, Rosebud. This is about me liking you and you liking me, slow dances to fast songs and not going down without a fight. You promised me you wouldn't go down without a fight, and I'm going to hold you to that."

As hard as she was biting it, she had to be putting a hole in that lip. A blotchy red blush broke over her face, and for a second, she didn't look that different from when he'd driven her home—just miserable.

"Have dinner with me tonight." It wasn't much, but he had to do something to get her to stop being so mule-stubborn. And he owed her a better ending—if she'd let him give her one.

"Or?"

He gaped at her. The way she said it made it sound like he was holding something over her head. "Or I'll eat alone?"

She forcibly swiveled her chair away from his and picked up her pen again. He waited. He'd pushed this just about as far as it was going to go, and whatever she said next was going to have to stand—for the time being, anyway.

"I can't."

Which was a hell of a lot different from an *I won't*. "What if I found some neutral territory?"

Her eyebrows jumped and she winced. "Neutral?"

"You can't come to my place, I know. You don't want me at your place. Obviously, local bars are a no-go...." He reached out and traced a finger along her bandage. She scrunched her eyes shut, and he thought she might be on the verge of crying. "Someplace quiet." His finger trailed down the rest of her face until he was running his thumb over her cheeks. He wanted to kiss her, but this wasn't the time or the place. "That's all I want. Just you and me."

"What makes you think it would be any different the next time?" Her voice shook as she blinked rapidly and pulled away from him. "Or the time after that? Or anytime? We can't hide forever. I can't, anyway."

Anger flashed through him. "I do *not* hide, Rosebud—and you shouldn't, either."

"You'd tell your uncle about this?" She pointed to her forehead, her eyes swimming. "About me?"

"No. I'm not stupid." He leaned back, frustrated with how lousy a job he was doing of convincing her. "Look. It's nobody's business when we see each other or what we do, and I want to keep it that way. I don't want to have to worry about what your aunt or my uncle or some moron on the street thinks about me or you or us." He'd like to kiss that lip she was hell-bent on chewing, but he didn't want to corner her. "It's like you said," he added, trying to back off a little, but not succeeding. He stroked her cheek again. "I'm just trying to stay out of the society pages. That's all."

Her whole face tensed, but then quickly relaxed as she leaned into his hand. Her eyelids fluttered. "Where?"

"Do you know where Bonneau Creek is?" At least, he thought that was what the map said. She nodded, so he must have said it right. "I think there's a cabin near there. No roads, no wires. Nothing else around for miles."

"That's almost ten miles away. I can't ride there tonight."

"What about this weekend? Will you spend it with me?"

The words hung in the air, and he realized exactly what he'd asked. Not dinner, not dancing, but the whole weekend—nights included.

Say yes, he thought.

Her hand covered his. She was shaking, just a little. "You won't tell anyone?"

His heart jumped. "Not even on my dying day."

She turned her head and kissed his palm. "Don't make me hold you to that," she said as she shot him a sly look and then pushed his chair away. Her meaning was clear—*Yes. Now get back to work.*

A yes was a yes. Despite the world's worst date, she'd still said yes. He was probably grinning like an idiot, but he didn't care. Even though he was an Armstrong, she actually liked him a whole lot—enough to come away for a weekend. "Don't worry. I won't."

Except for when her aunt Emily came in to check on her and to thank Dan for all the cookies, they worked in near silence for the rest of the day. Rosebud kept a safe distance from him above the table, but underneath, she rested one bare foot on his thigh.

Friday seemed a hell of a long way off.

Five days later, as he rode Smokey toward Bonneau Creek, the first thing Dan noticed was the way the world hushed around him. The silence wasn't something that came down like a hammer, but instead seemed to sneak up on him until he couldn't hear anything but the sound of Smokey's legs cutting through the tall grass. No birds. No bugs. Not even the wind blew.

A twig snapped. Dan zeroed in on the noise. About a hundred yards over his right shoulder, on the same deer path he'd heard it the first time. He grinned. She'd come. Keeping his ear focused on the spot, he carefully turned Smokey.

He blinked. Instead of his Indian princess, Rosebud sat astride her paint, buried within the shadows of the wood. Her horse took one more step out of the woods and into the sunlight. Her hair hung in a long, loose braid draped over her shoulder underneath a straw cowboy hat. She had on a plain white tank top, jeans and boots this time.

Same smile, though. She trotted down to him, and he took the time to appreciate the way her body moved. "Hi."

He leaned over as far as he could in the saddle and kissed her. Honey sweet—he wondered if the rest of her tasted the same. "I thought you were beautiful the first time, but I think I like you even better like this. More modern."

Her mouth opened and shut while she gave him a hell of a look. Yup—she was biting her inner lip again. He was getting a little tired of his former hat coming between them. Dan wished she'd just tell him the truth—and *why* would be nice, while she was at it. Giving her time to get herself organized, he turned Smokey north. At a walk, it would take them an hour and a half to get to the cabin.

"Here's what I don't understand," she said as her paint came parallel with him. "*If* you think that I took that shot, why are you here with me now?"

"I don't *think*." The horses fell into an easy stride, and he gave Smokey his head. They'd made this journey every night this week in preparation—although sometimes Dan took a different route, just in case. Smokey knew where they were going. "I *know*."

"If I took that shot," she repeated with more force.

Stubborn to the very end, he thought with a smile. He'd sort of thought that saving her at the bar might have gotten him a little more in the trust department, but he wasn't really surprised. "My mother always says, 'Most every person has a reason.'"

"And you think *that person* who took the shot had a reason?"

Dan's eyes swept along the valley and over the woman at his side. Her hips swiveled with every step her horse took, and her chest was a thing of beauty in slow motion. She held the tail end of the reins in her free hand, against her thigh. The sun glittered off her bare arms, but his eyes kept coming back to her face. No forced smiles, no dangerous stares. Just Rosebud, as nature intended. She belonged here, by the river, on horseback—not in some stuffy suit in an ugly office.

Most every person had a reason. He'd made it through all the police reports for vandalism on the rez in the past seven months. What had she said, back at the beginning? "What if *that person* had reason to believe they were shooting at someone who had 'engaged in a campaign of intimidation against members of the tribe'—that's what you said, right?" He knew now that was lawyer-speak for someone had been slashing tires and leaving bloody animal parts on her doorstep. She'd given him the files, but he hadn't asked her about the dead animals yet.

She was silent. He forced himself not to look at her. She'd spook easy right now, and that wasn't what led to a good weekend. But he wanted to know—he had to know—before they took this date to the next level. "That would be…a reason, but I'm sure *that person* wasn't trying to hit you. I'm sure *that person* was just trying to scare you off. I'm sure it was a mistake—*just* a mistake."

Lawyers, he thought with a snort. Still, this was progress. At least they were talking about it—without blanket denials. "*That person* needs to work on her aim. Scared the hell out of me—and Smokey." Smokey bobbed his head in agreement.

In the distance, he could see the river bend. After that, it was less than a mile until Bonneau Creek fed into the Dakota. They were halfway there.

Part of him—the part that needed to keep her safe— wanted to ask her if she knew who Shane Thrasher was, if that was who she'd thought she'd shot. But the part of him that was going to spend the weekend hidden away from the world with his Indian princess—that part held him back.

They couldn't do anything about Thrasher right now anyway. No need to ruin the moment.

"I'm sorry," she said unexpectedly. Her voice was soft and shaky, he thought, like she was making a confession. "I'll pay for your new hat. It's a nice one."

Now he did look at her. She was holding the reins so tight that her knuckles were white, and she was blinking at an unnaturally fast clip. It wasn't much of a confession, but it was something more than she'd given him before. "It won't happen again, will it?"

"No."

That was the truth, he could tell. Finally, there wasn't anything else between them. He reached over and rubbed her arm. He had her word, and that was good enough for him. "It's all right." She gave him a hesitant smile. Maybe she didn't believe him? "It really is. It was just a hat." It was nice of her to offer to pay for his new one, but she probably didn't have an extra thousand bucks lying around.

"It was almost your head." Her eyes were wet as she looked at him.

He held up a hand to cut her off. "It's done and over, and dwelling doesn't do anyone any good. I know you now. I know you're not some cold-blooded killer." He stood up in the stirrups to get closer to her. Smokey came to a confused halt, and Rosebud's paint followed suit. Dan was planning on hauling Rosebud over to him, but he didn't have to. She met him halfway, grabbing a handful of his shirt to brace him. "I trust you, Rosebud."

He was semibalanced about a foot away from her face. He wanted to kiss her, but he was afraid he might head-butt her at this angle. Her cheeks prettied up, but she held his gaze—and his shirt. "I shouldn't trust you," she said, looking coy and embarrassed at the same time.

"But?"

"But I do." She shot forward, and he felt her lips graze his cheek before she let go. He sat back down in the saddle hard, but he couldn't tear his eyes away from her. "I can't seem to help myself when it comes to you," she said.

Now *that* sounded like a good weekend in the making. "Good. Now, I want to see you ride that horse." He touched his heels to Smokey's side and picked up speed. "Come on, darlin'," he called over his shoulder. "Let's get gone!"

She let out a "Yeah!" and came thundering up behind him. The weekend had officially begun.

Twelve

Feeling lighter than she had in a long time, Rosebud watched as Dan built the campfire with his bare hands as the sun set lazily behind the woods. She'd apologized—without actually admitting any wrongdoing—and he'd forgiven her. She was on a vacation of sorts. She hadn't had a true day off since last Christmas, and she felt giddy about spending it with—whoa. He took his T-shirt off and used it to fan the fire.

Holy cow, Dan shirtless was about a thousand times better than Dan clothed—and he was pretty damn fine with his shirt on. She must have whistled, because his head popped up and he shot her a grin that walked a fine line between snarky and sultry. Was she really doing this? Running away for the weekend with a white man—an Armstrong, no less? It was one thing to get swept away while dancing at a bar—but this? This was a certain kind of crazy. Rationally, she knew she shouldn't trust him. But *rational* had nothing to do with anything anymore.

For a second, she felt horrible that she'd missed out on this last week. She rubbed the small Band-Aid on her forehead. Nope. Not thinking about it. She had too much else to think about right now—like Dan hauling a bucket of water up from the creek for the horses. Wow. Muscles in action.

She was staring. Again. Dan brushed the horses, a true cowboy to the core. His hands moved the brush over each muscle with due diligence. Logically, she knew the horses had to be cooled down before they could get on with their evening, but she didn't know how much longer she could wait for him.

The weight between her legs was heavy, and the tension of holding in sheer, unadulterated desire was wearing her out. The ride out here had gotten her blood pumping, and Dan doing chores kept it pumping. She tore her eyes away from his bare torso and dug her condoms out of her bag.

No nightstand. Hmm. The bed was one of those old-fashioned foldable things on metal springs, but the sheets were fresh and surprisingly soft. Much softer than the ones she had at home. God, how much would that thing squeak? Finally, she decided to put the condoms just under the bed—within reach, but not exactly in line of sight. She might only have another three weeks with Dan—she had to make it count. After the court date, she had no idea what would happen. She found herself hoping he would stay, but she was afraid he was itching to get back to Texas.

Condoms tucked away, she straightened up as she heard him kick off his boots at the door. If she turned around, she might just throw herself at him, so she stayed put. "You've been busy."

Dan wrapped his arms around her waist and pulled her back into his chest. He smelled of horse and wood smoke, with just a little of that sandalwood. He whipped off his hat and threw it onto the only other piece of furniture in the room, a rickety table. She officially didn't care how much the bed would squeak. "Not the penthouse or anything, but how do you like it?" His voice was low and close to her ear. Then he kissed her neck.

Which *it* was that—the cabin, the man in it or what she wanted to do to that man? Didn't matter. "I love it."

"I brought dinner." His stubble scratched over her ear as his arms tightened around her waist. One hand splayed out just below her breast, the other found her hip, and they were dancing again, slow and sweet. The heat from his chest made her shirt stick to her back. "If you're hungry."

Keeping time with the silent rhythm of their bodies, she turned in his arms. His eyes locked on to hers. The scent of sex seemed to pour off his skin, filling the room. "I didn't come here for dinner."

"Me neither." This time, he didn't wait for permission, and he didn't hold back. His lips fastened onto hers with a driving need that must have tripped another wire in her brain, because all of a sudden she was yanking his belt free and he was peeling her shirt off and the next thing she knew, the bed was squeaking. Loudly.

She couldn't help but giggle at the horrific noise. Anyplace else, and she'd be mortified that someone somewhere would hear them. But not here. She lifted her hips as he worked her jeans and panties off. She had no idea where her bra had gone, but in less than a minute, she was nude before him.

A lone finger traced down between her aching breasts to just below her belly. *"Damn."* The moment her legs were free of all unnecessary fabric, she sat up and began unbuttoning his jeans. The bed wailed in protest of all this movement, which set off another round of giggling, but then she froze. She hoped he didn't think she was giggling at *him*.

"It's okay." His voice was thick with strain as he grabbed at his back pocket before she could shuck his pants entirely. He pulled out a condom and tore it open with his teeth. He'd planned ahead, too. Could this man get any more perfect? "I kind of like it a little loud."

"Yeah?" Briefs. Not that they stayed on for long.

He was—well, not *huge* per se, but firmly into the *well-endowed* category. Very firmly. He rolled the condom on and then knelt on the bed between her legs. The whole thing shuddered, and Dan paused to grip both sides of the mattress. The anticipation was going to kill her if the bed didn't do her in first. "Maybe we should—"

Nope. Not waiting another minute. She grabbed his face and hauled him down to her as she wrapped her legs around his waist. She wanted to lick every inch of him until the taste of his musk was burned into her memory. She wanted to feel every inch of him until her hands had memorized every muscle. *Make it count,* she prayed.

He pulled away, his chest heaving as he tested out the bed. It held. "Easy."

"I don't want it easy." Her fingers scraped over his chest and around to his backside. She pulled him toward her, toward the heaviness that was driving her mad. The slickness of the condom touched her, but having that dull weight on the outside wasn't doing her any favors. "I want you. Now."

Moving slow enough not to flip the bed, he reached down between her legs and touched her center. His fingers spread her wide. He was against her, then in her. Her body convulsed. "Is this what you want?"

"Yes," she moaned, shimmying around his width. He pulled back—almost out—and a whimper escaped her lips.

"This?" He drove all the way in, his head bowing over hers until their foreheads were touching. Panting, his breath surrounded her. He surrounded her, filled her. She was safe, here in his arms. Nothing and no one could hurt her.

He was everything she'd hoped, but nothing like she'd imagined. Better. So much better. *"Dan."*

He pulled back again and paused. What was he waiting for? "Tell me what you want." His voice was stretched thin, like he was just barely holding on to the edge of a steep cliff.

Her hips shimmied again, hoping to draw him back in. "Loud?" Because what he wanted was what she wanted.

"Yeah." He moved in small circles, just inside her. He was toying with her, damn it.

"Harder." He buried himself with more force, and her cry broke free. "Oh!"

He made a noise in the back of his throat, an instinctive growl that was pleasure and hunger and satisfaction all rolled into one. But again, he pulled back, slow and steady.

Her orgasm was so close, but it was stuck behind a wall of three years of waiting for this exact moment. Dan had to break through that wall, he just *had* to. Slow and steady wasn't the way. "Faster," she demanded, smacking the flat of her hand on his behind. "Harder. Faster."

He grunted, his body picking up wonderful speed. Each thrust did make her louder. He was driving into her with a passion—a force—that she'd never felt before. All the wires in her brain tripped, and before she knew it, she was shouting his name in time with each meeting of their bodies.

"Can't…hold on…long," he got out through clenched teeth.

He drove in again, but this time his lips found hers. The final, intimate touch shattered the wall around her. *Dan!* But the word didn't come. All that came was a scream that he seemed to swallow whole. He exploded in a flurry of hurried thrusts before his head flew back and he made a noise closer to a mountain lion roaring than a man coming. He shivered through a final half thrust and fell on top of her.

The bed was silent while she tried to catch her breath with his weight on top of her. Sated, she ran the pads of her fingers over his back more slowly now, taking her time to really feel him.

"Oh, Rosebud." His voice was muffled against her neck—and then he started kissing her skin. "I—you—"

She was afraid to open her mouth, because her head was buzzing with all the circuits he'd not only tripped, but blown completely. However, when his lips moved over her collarbone and began to make their way to her bare breasts, she started to giggle.

His head popped up, and the bed creaked. "Rosebud?"

"Oh, no, not you—I just— Oh, my God—you were amazing. I've been wanting—since that first time—on the horse—I mean—just, you know, that was amazing. Not that—*you*—you were—*are*—amazing." Yup. Circuits blown. She was babbling.

He propped himself up on one hand and grinned at her. "Interesting." He sounded amused, which was probably the best she could hope for. "So, what you're sayin' is, you liked it."

"Uh-huh." She couldn't even get that out without another round of giggles as he swung his legs over the bed. She rolled over and traced the shape of his shoulder blades. No, she decided, he couldn't get any more perfect.

"And you wouldn't mind doin' it again a little later?"

"Not *too* much later."

That made him laugh, and despite the bed's protests, he reached around, picked her up—actually picked her up—and sat her on his lap. He kissed her forehead, her cheeks, her eyelids. "Can you wait half an hour?"

Finally, she felt a little bit of sanity returning to her brain. "I suppose I don't have much choice, do I?" She needed to get cleaned up. Some recovery time would probably be good for both of them.

At that moment, Rosebud realized there was no bathroom in the cabin.

Dan laughed again, a satisfied sound rounded out by happiness. "You've got your choice of the tree to the left, or the bush to the right."

She stretched out on his lap, and his hands slid over her bare flesh. "Bush." She'd peed behind both trees and bushes, and the bush held the promise of slightly more coverage.

By the time she got her clothes back on, Dan was crouched before the fire. A plush blanket was spread out on the ground and over some old stumps, giving them someplace to sit. Dinner was the best cold fried chicken and biscuits she'd ever eaten. Then he broke out the marshmallows and chocolate wrapped in gold foil. "S'mores?" That chocolate looked far too expensive to waste on graham crackers.

"We're camping," he replied, stripping a stick and handing it to her. By now, the sun had set, and the only light for miles around was a crescent moon and the fire. "I think there's a law that says if you've got a campfire, you've got to make s'mores." Stripping his own stick, he sat down next to her.

With the light flickering over his face, he looked a whole lot more like the little boy in the poster than the man who ran Armstrong Holdings. "Far be it from me to argue with the law. Or chocolate. Pass the marshmallows."

By the time she'd set three marshmallows on fire, he was snickering like a boy, too. "What am I going to do with you?" he asked as he blew out another victim.

"That's sort of a good question." One she'd love to know the answer to.

He paused in the middle of squeezing his perfectly melted marshmallow between the chocolate and graham crackers, and then handed her the finished product. "You got all serious on me there."

She tried to laugh it off. "Sorry. I haven't had a day off in a long time. It's hard to shut off my brain."

He skewered another marshmallow, but he didn't roast it. He stared at the fire in silence for such a long time that she was sure she'd pushed him too far—although she didn't see how. Finally, he pivoted on his heels and stared at her.

"Rosebud," he said in such a serious voice that for a second, she was afraid he was going to do something completely irrational and ask for her hand in marriage. Her heart started to thud. "What if there was no reservoir?"

Thirteen

"What?" she gasped, scooting away from Dan. "What do you mean, no reservoir?"

Mistake, he thought. He shouldn't have tried to mix business with what had been an unabashed pleasure up to that point. "I'm going to bring my engineer up here in a few weeks." She stopped scooting, her eyes trained on him with a laserlike focus. At least he had her undivided attention. "I've been studying the plans. We could do a run-of-river dam."

She sucked in air like it was going out of style. Then she sprang to her feet, hovering between backing up some more and maybe grabbing him by his lapels and shaking him senseless. "*We* could do a *what?*"

"A run-of-river couldn't store electricity for when the river's low, but it wouldn't require a reservoir. The difference is only a few thousand—way less than Cecil's spent on lawyers the last few years." He stood, but slowly. He didn't want to spook her—any more than he'd already spooked her.

"You—the dam—no?" She spun around, stalked off into the darkness, and was back in the circle of light in a heartbeat. "We?"

As the firelight danced over the flustered planes of her face, his mind flashed back to the sex. She'd lost all control—he'd seen her do it twice now. Her mouth ran a mile a minute when it happened, good or bad. This? This was good. She had one hand over her heart, the other waving in his general direction. Way more than half an hour had passed, and he couldn't wait to get her good and flustered all over again.

"I'm not makin' any promises—I've got to get Jimmy up here to look it over—but it's *possible.* That's all." He took her hand and pulled her into his arms. Man, she just *fit,* all warm and soft and sweet.

"No flooding?" He could feel her heart racing against his chest.

He shook his head. "I don't trust Cecil's engineering firm any more than I trust Cecil. They've got to have an ulterior motive for pushing the reservoir, but I don't know what it is."

"Dan—you mean it? No dam?"

"I didn't say that. I said *maybe* no reservoir. Look," he said, taking her face in his hands. "This is Cecil's deal—but it's still my company, and the *company* has sunk a lot of money into this. I can't afford to walk away from the deal."

He could see the wheels in her mind spinning. His own wheels were picking up speed. A lot of things had to go right—like wrestling control of this project, and eventually the company, away from Cecil, for starters—but he'd spent his every waking moment for the past few weeks either being near Rosebud or thinking about being near her. She didn't make it easy on him, but somehow, being with her was the kind of difficult that a man could get used to.

She opened her mouth to say something, but nothing came out. The only sound she made was a small squeak.

Not just any woman would consider run-of-river dams foreplay. But if he'd learned anything, it was that Rosebud wasn't just any woman. He tightened his arms around her, enjoying the way she rubbed against him as he leaned down to kiss her. "Yeah, I thought that's what you'd say."

Her honey sweetness was tempered with chocolate this time, and it only made him want to kiss her more. She ran her hands over his five o'clock shadow as she licked his lips. Oh, yeah, the half hour was up, and so was he. He growled in satisfaction as she ground her hips against him. Already he had her shirt half-off, but he couldn't make the move toward the bed. That damned thing was just too loud.

"I've been dreaming about this," she said as she whipped his shirt over his head and pushed him back down toward the blanket. The cool night air just made him want to get warm the old-fashioned way.

He dug another condom out of his back pocket before he lost his pants again. Man, but she was fast with those buttons. "Yeah?" Her mouth was running. This was going to be good.

"After that first kiss—you and me—by the river—*dreaming*," she repeated.

She pushed him down to the ground, and with an agonizingly slow pace, undid her jeans. In the firelight, the peaks of her nipples gleamed like rubbed copper. Her hips swiveled as she worked them free of her jeans, and then she undid her braid. Her hair fell free around her in loose waves. She jutted out that chin and squared her shoulders, showing none of that typical self-consciousness that always had women turning out lights or wrapping up in robes. No, she was a proud Indian princess, and she'd brought the cowboy to his knees.

"Damn, darlin'." Her mouth might be going, but his was freezing up. All he could do was stare and wait for her.

As she lowered herself onto him, her wetness surrounding

everything he had to offer her, she scraped her breasts over his stubble and groaned.

The sound of her making love to him was enough to send him right over the edge all by itself. The first time he'd been with a woman who liked it loud had been like his very first time all over again. Something about a woman who didn't hold back drove him wild. "You like that?" Because if she was driving him wild, he wanted to make damn sure she came driving with him.

"Oh, yeah." She arched her back, thrusting those all-natural beauties into his face. Her hair pooled down behind her, covering them both in a blanket of black silk. "So good. So— *Oh!*"

His mouth fastened to her nipple, Dan couldn't help but smile as she bucked so hard he had to grab her around the waist to keep her from falling off him. Holding her to him with one hand, he sucked as hard as he could on one breast and let his fingers do the tugging on the other.

Her hands grabbed his hair and held on. Her nipples were rock hard in his mouth, and each pass of his tongue or his teeth or his stubble—especially his stubble—upped her volume. Finally, Dan couldn't take it anymore. He had to come, and he had to come right now. He grabbed her hips and pumped in as hard and as fast as he could, the sounds of her screaming his name into the wide-open night putting him in a place he'd only just glimpsed before. Her noise—her plea-sure—blotted out everything else, even the coppery glow of her skin. All he could see and feel, taste and touch, was the sound of what he was doing to her.

He couldn't remember ever coming as hard as she made him come.

By the time the rest of his senses caught up with him, she had her head buried into the crook of his neck. She was sort of moaning, sort of whimpering, but the meaning was the same.

"Yeah." Which was not some of his better pillow talk, but it was all he had left. "Me, too."

He didn't want to let her go, but the night air came down hard on them now that they weren't actively keeping it away. Moving wasn't easy. He was six kinds of tired, and at least that many kinds of satisfied. By the time he got the fire out, she'd pulled the mattress to the floor and curled up in the bed.

"A woman after my own heart." Exhaustion clawed at him as he crawled in next to her. Tiffany had never stayed the night—her choice. Staying meant a more permanent thing, she'd told him once, and Dan could never do permanent. She'd been right—then.

Now?

Rosebud snuggled up against his side—she didn't have much of a choice, the bed wasn't that big—and draped a leg over his. Now, this close tangle of legs and arms and skin seemed more permanent than anything he'd ever felt for a woman.

"You never answered the question." Her voice managed to beat back the sleepy darkness, but just barely.

"What question?"

"What *are* you going to do with me?"

More permanent, he thought, finding her fingers and lacing them with his. Sleep could not be denied much longer, but he didn't want to leave her hanging. "I'm thinking about keeping you."

By the time Sunday rolled around, Dan was doing a lot more thinking. Sure, he'd gone camping plenty of times—but he couldn't remember ever liking it as much as he did with Rosebud around. Maybe it was because he hadn't gone camping since he'd taken control of the petroleum division ten years ago—it was hard to pitch a tent in a tie. Maybe it was because she liked the stuff he liked—riding the horses after breakfast, taking a skinny dip in the afternoon and cuddling by the campfire at night. Maybe it was because they made sweet, sleepy love in the morning and had screaming hot sex by moonlight. Maybe it was because she couldn't roast a marshmallow if her life depended on it. Whatever it was, by the time they packed up and headed out, he was already figuring out the plans for next weekend.

"We should take a different route," he said when they got back to where the Bonneau Creek fed into the Dakota.

"Why?" She kept close to him—not close enough to crowd the horses, but close enough that he could still reach out and touch her arm.

"Because—" His brain bit back the words *I might be followed* before they got all the way out.

"Dan," she said, and he knew by the tone of her voice that he hadn't been fast enough. "*Why* do we need to take a different route?"

At least the weekend had already been great. He wouldn't ruin the whole thing now. "Do you know who Shane Thrasher is?"

"No." He swore that, even though they were still riding, she froze. "Should I?"

Damn his big mouth. She'd gotten him all relaxed and comfortable, and this was what popped out. "He's Cecil's 'head of security,'" he said, using air quotes. "And he's half Crow."

She sucked in air hard, but managed to keep her game face on. He didn't like her game face. He liked her real face. "And he's tailing—you? Me? Us?"

"I'm not sure, but it's possible he's tailing me. I haven't seen any other tracks, so I'm sure he hasn't found our cabin." Given the way she was getting all splotchy on him over there, he'd better be damn sure, but he'd checked around the campsite every time they left and every time they came back, and had seen no signs of anyone or thing. No cigarette butts. Not even a questionable hoofprint. "Better safe than sorry, though. I don't want him to find our place."

They rode north for a little bit before they came to a wide spot in the river. When he turned Smokey into the water, Rosebud finally spoke up. "You're scaring me."

He shot her a confused look. "It's real shallow here. I've come this way twice. Won't even get your boots wet."

"That's not what I mean." She looked over her shoulder, and he saw the fear. "What if..."

"No one saw us. No one will see us," he promised, suddenly wishing he'd checked a little more thoroughly. All that screaming... "And I won't let anyone scare you. That's a promise, Rosebud." She gave him a worried smile, one that said she wasn't really convinced. "I mean it. Anyone messes with you, and I'll shoot them myself."

She took another long look around, but the river valley was the same wild, untouched place it had been before he'd been dumb enough to bring up Thrasher. "That won't be necessary," she finally said as they crossed the river. "I can take care of myself."

That all-business tone of voice was what worried him the most. "Will you still come away with me next weekend?"

She looked to the heavens, as if that was where the answer lay. "I shouldn't." His heart dropped a pained notch or two, but then she sighed and added, "If we leave real early Saturday morning, no one will know where we went."

"Darlin,' I'll go anywhere, anytime, as long as I'm with you."

She twisted in the saddle and shot him a look that was a

whole lot of knowing and a little bit of longing. He waited for her to say something, but she didn't.

She just rode away from him. He had to hurry to catch up.

Fourteen

"Where were you this weekend?" Cecil didn't look like he'd moved from his desk since last Thursday, the last time Dan had seen him.

Dan bristled. For a split second, he felt like a hormonal teenager busted for being out past curfew. "Out." He didn't owe Cecil anything more than that, but the monosyllabic response caused the man to look up.

"Who with?"

"My horse. I rode down south to check out a few things on the map." As far as he could tell, there wasn't much down south except scrub grass and a lonely, forgotten cell phone tower. South would be a good direction for Shane Thrasher to go to get lost. Maybe he'd be eaten by a coyote.

Something about Cecil changed. He went from his normal pissed look to something that was supposed to be warm and inviting—if one liked eels. "So," he said, his tone suddenly all buddy-buddy. "How are things going with that Donnelly woman?"

Dan would rather chew off his own arm in a bear trap than give away anything about his Indian princess. "I don't know what you think I can do with her. She's real easy on the eyes, but she doesn't take anything from anyone—me included. I can't even get her to dinner again. She caught wind of my scheme that first time and won't even look at me. It's like I'm not even there."

"No progress, huh." Dan took the mild look of disappointment as a compliment. Cecil was actually buying that load of bull crap. The old man flipped to a calendar and thought. "We've got less than three weeks until that court date. Keep at her, son. Even the toughest nuts can be cracked."

So help him, the only thing Dan could think of cracking was Cecil, right across the mouth. "Why are we pushing the reservoir? Why aren't we doing a run-of-river?"

"Do you have any idea how much money we've sunk into this?" Cecil slapped his hand on the desk in an unnecessary show of force.

Dan didn't flinch. "*We* didn't." He kept his voice calm and level—his COO voice, Mom always said. His cut-the-crap voice was how he thought of it. "*You* did."

For the blink of an eye, Cecil actually looked surprised. But the contempt washed away everything else real quick. "Don't tell me you're listening to that woman. For Christ's sake, she's a lunatic! A raving lunatic who's cost this company millions of dollars!"

"Seems to me you may be the one costing this company millions. I'm going to be bringing some of my people in— *my* engineer, *my* audit team. We're going to need to review *your* books, Cecil."

Surprise flashed over his face again, but this time he looked more cornered. "I should have known bringing you up here was a mistake. You're too soft for this business. Just like your mother." The words weren't even sharp enough to cut, not with the way his voice wavered.

Dan had the old man trapped, and they both knew it. "I'll be sure to mention you to her. She does enjoy hearing what you're up to, being as her vote carries such weight with the board."

Cecil blanched. "You can audit your ass off, but we're breaking ground in three weeks."

Nothing but bluster. Chances were decent that Rosebud was going to get her injunction, and Dan needed the stay to get his team organized. He wanted his top guys and gals up here, but they were all hip-deep in various other projects. Three weeks out was the earliest he could pull everyone out of Texas without compromising the other jobs.

And he needed that time to figure out what Cecil was up to. If he couldn't prove that Cecil was doing anything illegal, then the board would have no reason to force the old man out. Dan turned on his heels and headed for his room.

How was he going to get Cecil out of the picture? He needed hard evidence. But what?

Dan was emptying his bag out and rounding up the dirty laundry when it hit him.

Maria.

She was in the kitchen, humming as she rolled tamales. He hadn't checked for bugs since he'd had dinner here with Rosebud, so he made up some lame excuse about wanting to check her tire pressure to get her out of the house.

"Maria," he asked as he bent over her tires, "who do you work for? Me, or Cecil?"

"Señor Cecil," she replied after a long minute. "But I would like to work for you." Her voice was so quiet that he almost couldn't hear it over the faint rush of air that escaped the tire gauge. "You are a better man, *señor*."

"Well, I'm hiring." Going through the motions, they moved

around to the other tire. "I'm looking for something. A lock-box that Cecil keeps separate from his other files."

"I'm not allowed in his office, *señor*." They moved to the back tires. "What does it look like?"

Dan hid his grin. He was definitely hiring. "It's made of wood—oak, I think—and it looks real old. He had a key with it—small. Silver, I think." One more tire to go. "It had a file in it that he marked up with a red pen."

"I have not seen such a thing before." The tires were done. Maria straightened. "Thank you for checking." Then, under her breath, she added, "I will look."

"Yeah, just tell Eduardo to keep an eye on that front one," he said a little louder than he meant to as they walked back into the house.

The number of Armstrong Holdings employees in South Dakota had just gone up by one.

"Rosebud?" Aunt Emily was sitting in her chair, the quilt square spread out before her. "Honey, where have you been?"

"Out." Which was the lamest of all possible excuses. She'd lived with Aunt Emily for so long that they really didn't have secrets. "I just needed a weekend off. I've been so busy with the dam...."

Aunt Emily looked at her, at her backpack, then back at her before she turned her eyes back to her work. She wasn't buying it, but Rosebud wasn't about to crack. Maybe when she'd been a teenager, she could be intimidated by the knowing silence, but not anymore. She didn't have to explain herself to anyone—one of the fringe benefits of being an adult.

Rosebud set her bag down and began to make a peanut butter sandwich. Food had been secondary this weekend, and even the rumble in her belly was enough to make her smile in contentment. *Dan.* Just thinking his name was enough to make her shiver. Still, the sandwich hit the spot.

Rosebud was rummaging in the fridge to see if they had any apples when Aunt Emily's voice cut through her hazy happiness. "Have you gotten anything out of that Dan Armstrong yet?"

The hackles on the back of her neck shot up. All her training kicked in, and Rosebud went on the offensive before she knew what she was doing. "I don't know what you think I'm going to 'get' out of him," she snapped as she slammed the fridge door. "He doesn't know anything about dams, and from what I can tell, Cecil keeps him clueless." All statements that were true three weeks ago. Now? Everything was different. Which made it official. She was lying to her aunt. Something she had never done before.

And to make things worse, they both knew it. Aunt Emily looked at her with a sense of confused wonder on her face. "He doesn't know anything."

It should have been a question, but it wasn't. Aunt Emily was just repeating the bald-faced lie as a matter of statement.

Guilt smacked Rosebud upside the head, and for a second, she wanted to tell Aunt Emily about the run-of-river option. Rosebud had done what she was supposed to, after all. She'd gotten into Dan's head, muddled his thinking and made him see her side. Aunt Emily would be proud of her. Except that wasn't why Rosebud was doing it. At this point, the dam was almost secondary. Almost.

Rosebud looked Aunt Emily in the eye. "No." The lie came easier this time. Part of it was self-preservation. Maybe this thing with Dan was only a weekend thing. Maybe he'd go back to Texas in three weeks. Maybe he'd stay around long enough to see her rez at the bottom of a lake. She didn't want people thinking she'd lost her head and sunk the tribe over a man, over an Armstrong.

Or maybe it would all work out. The chances were slim, but the element of surprise was key. If Cecil got wind of what

Dan and Rosebud were up to, the run-of-river option might fall apart. She'd be lucky if *just* the rez went under. It would all be on her head.

Aunt Emily held her gaze for a year-long moment before the older woman sighed and turned back to her quilting. "Be careful, Rosebud."

If her hackles stood up any more, they'd rip themselves right off her neck. "What's that supposed to mean? When am I not careful?" Her mind flashed back to the look on Dan's face when he'd told her they should take a different route to the cabin next time. The peanut butter sandwich felt like a lead weight in her belly.

Aunt Emily clucked at her. At least she wasn't staring Rosebud down anymore. "You can't forget who he is. Who you are. Who you represent." Rosebud thought for a second that Aunt Emily was about to launch into the history of the tribe, just like she did when Rosebud wanted her to wear down an opponent.

For one wonderful weekend, Rosebud had managed to forget exactly who she represented. For two days, there had been no Armstrong Holdings and no Red Creek tribe. For two days, she hadn't felt like she had the weight of the world on her shoulders. For two wonderful, freeing days, she'd been happy for the first time in so long…since before Tanner died. She couldn't help it—even now, she wanted nothing more than to go back to where it was just Dan and Rosebud.

And that alone was enough to make her one of "them" instead of one of "us."

"I know what I'm doing," she managed to get out. Which was not the same as knowing what she was *supposed* to be doing. But she was damn tired of living her life for someone—everyone—else. Was it too much to ask to do what she wanted for once?

Aunt Emily shook her head in what looked a hell of a lot like disappointment.

Rosebud focused all of her energy on not slamming the door to her room. She knew what she was doing.

Next weekend, she was going to the cabin with Dan.

Fifteen

Rosebud sat across the table, staring at Dan. She could tell he knew she was staring, because he kept grinning as he handed over sheet after sheet of official company biography. "And Jim Evans—he's my chief engineer. They'll all be coming up together in two weeks—the day after the hearing, actually. If Jim gets done with his current project, he might make it in earlier, but I can't guarantee that."

A small part of her was immensely relieved that he really was flying up his own team. She had been worried silly that Dan had just been whispering sweet nothings in her ear because he wanted to get her into a compromising position. But he was nothing if not serious about it—and he had the itineraries to prove it. "They aren't going to be staying with you, are they?"

"I don't think Cecil is open to that option," he replied, answering the correct question. But then his face got dark—the same look he'd gotten when he'd asked her about Thrasher. He flipped a piece of paper over and began scribbling.

He doesn't like you. Dan's handwriting was borderline atrocious, but she could still make it out.

Big shock there. *Aunt Emily's not a big fan of you, either,* she wrote back.

Dan sighed, like he'd been hoping for a better outcome. *I kind of hate this sneaking around thing,* he wrote back.

Me, too. But I don't know how to get around it.

He looked at her, and she saw something in his eyes that wasn't like and wasn't even lust. She'd never seen that look before—on anyone—and the intensity of it gave her goose bumps. "What?"

I'm working on it, he wrote. *Be careful.*

I will, she promised.

Careful was harder than it sounded. For one thing, Rosebud and Aunt Emily weren't exactly on speaking terms, which made dinner every night awkward. All that awkwardness spilled over to the office. Judy could tell something was wrong, and began acting like it was her job on the line.

For another thing, every day Rosebud saw Dan made it that much harder to keep her hands off him. They both knew that there could be no touching and certainly no kissing anywhere they might get caught. No temptation allowed, period.

But Dan had the nerve to let his stubble get a little closer to a full beard, until just the sight of his face made her ache in good ways. She had wild fantasies about stripping for him at the office and doing all sorts of crazy things on the conference table—even on the wobbly chair. All the unresolved tension nearly gave her a tummy ache.

Careful also required that they take long and winding routes to the cabin both weekends—so long that, by the time they got there, it took everything she had not to rip his shirt off.

But once they were at the cabin, *careful* was the last thing on their minds. She had been afraid that there was no way the sex could top the excitement of that first weekend, but Dan took great pleasure in proving her wrong. The first time he went down on her, scraping his near-beard over her breasts, down her belly and between her thighs, she screamed so loudly that she lost her voice.

The first time he took her from behind and reached down between her legs from the front until he found her throbbing little spot, she came so hard that she accidentally knocked him off the mattress and onto the floor. But instead of being mad at her, he just rolled her onto her back and promised she wouldn't get away the next time.

The first time he gathered her into his arms after another explosive orgasm and said, "I think I'm falling for you, Rosebud," he brought her to tears—tears he kissed away.

"I think I'm falling for you, too." Which was, of course, a gross understatement of the situation. Rosebud didn't think—she knew she was falling in love with Dan. She was already in love with him.

"Just Dan and Rosebud," he said, sounding happy and solemn at the same time as the crickets chirped away outside. The world—their world—was calm and peaceful. "That's what I want. Just Dan and Rosebud."

Her breath caught in her throat. "That's what I want, too."

But they both knew it wasn't that simple.

"Dan coming in today?" Judy asked as the coffee perked.

Rosebud worked at keeping her face still, although she knew it was pointless. Dan—and her relationship with him—was sort of an open secret by now. No one could prove anything, but lots of people had noticed how much time the two of them had spent in the conference room in the past two and a half weeks. "I'm not sure," she said, trying to be convincing. "I don't know if I'll have time for him. The court date is tomorrow, after all." Judy was not convinced, to say the least. Rosebud sighed. "Let me know if he shows up, okay?"

"Of course," Judy replied with a wink.

Great, Rosebud thought. *So much for being careful.*

Tomorrow was the big day, although it was just another battle in the war. She was doing the final check on all her ducks. Each row had to be perfect. Dan had told her that if she got the preliminary injunction, the odds were decent that he could get control of the project by the time the order expired. Rosebud was itching to tell someone about their plan, but unfortunately, the plan included telling no one. Neither she nor Dan could afford to have their positions compromised. Things had to go off smoothly or they wouldn't go off at all.

She dove into her briefs, only vaguely aware that it was well past Dan's normal arrival time. He'd said he might have things to do—after all, his team was coming in this weekend—so she refused to spend much time thinking about it.

It wasn't until Judy knocked on her door that she realized it was half past ten. "Is he here?" she asked as she dug for her lipstick.

"No." The sheer terror in Judy's voice snapped Rosebud's head up. Judy was as pale as was physically possible. If Rosebud wasn't mistaken, the woman was on the verge of passing out.

"Who is it?" Her voice rang tinny in her own ears. Something was wrong.

"It's Cecil Armstrong."

Rosebud's blood ran middle-of-January cold. After all this time, *that man* had the nerve to show up? What the hell was he doing here? Where was Dan? *Snap out of it,* she ordered herself. Now was not the time to panic. "What does he want?"

"He wants to talk to you. And he's got another man with him. Not Dan."

"Did you get a name?"

"I think he said Shane Thrasher, but…" Judy waved her hands, which only seemed to spread a sense of panic around the room like an aerosol can. "He's got a gun. I can tell—I've seen those cop shows. Under his jacket."

"Oh, hell." Shane Thrasher. "Okay. Don't panic." Like that was even an option right now. Rosebud wasn't even sure her heart was still pumping. "Can you get them some coffee?"

Judy looked like she wanted to cry.

"Don't worry about it," Rosebud said before the water-works started. "Just get Joe. I don't care if you have to drag his butt out of bed—I want him to get that gun out of this building, okay?"

"Okay," Judy said and all but sprinted to her phone.

Rosebud wasn't much better. She grabbed her phone so fast she dropped it. "Come on," she said as Dan's number rang in her ear. "Pick up."

He didn't. The call went straight to voice mail. The panic in her belly ratcheted up a notch. Where the hell *was* he?

"Dan? It's Rosebud. Your uncle and Shane Thrasher are sitting in my conference room, and I don't know where you are. If you could…" Could what? Get the cavalry and ride to the rescue? Bust in here with both barrels blazing? "If you could just let me know if you know what's going on, I'd really appreciate it. I—" Her mouth snapped shut, biting the *love you* in half. No weakness. No confession. "Uh, I'll talk to you later, right? Bye."

She forced herself to go through her normal pre-meeting routine. Braided hair—check. Lipstick—check. Files in order—check. But there was no convincing herself. Nothing about this unscheduled meeting was normal, and that unavoidable fact had her stomach churning so fast she was nauseous.

After all this time, Cecil Armstrong had come to see her.

There was always a chance he'd come in peace, she thought as she buttoned up her suit jacket. Or maybe he was here to give up. Surrender would be nice.

Her pep talk failed to make her peppy.

"Rosie?" Joe White Thunder popped his head in the door. She jumped so hard that she almost knocked her chair over. "What's going on?"

"Oh, thank God." Joe was here. The whole world hadn't gone completely mad. "Cecil Armstrong is in the conference room with his head of security, a man named Shane Thrasher. Judy said she saw Thrasher's gun. I need you to make sure he gets it the hell out of here."

Joe stared at her for a long second in what could only be shock before he squared his shoulders. "I'll take care of him," he said, looking twenty years younger in an instant and sounding every inch the Lakota warrior.

Rosebud's heart was pounding so hard she was sure her whole body was visibly shaking. She did *not* want to go in that room before she knew where Dan was, but the longer she put it off, the more nervous she would become. She had to get this over with quick.

She stood with her hand on the doorknob, trying to get her body to respond to her orders. Joe put his hand on her shoulder and gave her a strong squeeze. "You can do this, Rosie," he whispered.

"Right." She still wasn't sure what *this* was, but she could do it. Taking a last breath of Cecil-free air, she opened the door to the conference room. *Into the abyss,* she thought.

Cecil Armstrong stood over the wobbly chair with a man who had to be Shane Thrasher on his hands and knees, looking at the undercarriage of the wounded seat. A small sense of victory calmed her nerves. She still had the upper hand.

Armstrong looked much like he did in the photos she'd found of him, but in person he seemed more shriveled,

more…yellow. Sallow, she thought, remembering the name
for it, like he never saw the sun. In her mind's eye, she had
always thought of him as this huge mountain of an obstacle
she had to conquer, but in person he was a good eight inches
shorter than Dan. Just an old, shriveled-up man, she thought.
The realization gave her strength. He had no power over her,
none at all. She was not afraid, and she was not going down
without a fight. It didn't matter that Dan wasn't here. She
was confident that he had a good reason for not answering
the phone. He probably didn't even know Cecil was here. She
and Dan had a plan, and she was going to stick with that plan,
come hell or high water.

"Mr. Armstrong, what a surprise." At least her voice was
listening to her orders. It came out strong and confident.
She turned to Thrasher, who was now standing. "And Mr.…
Thrasher, is it?"

Thrasher's eyes slid over her with cold familiarity. He
smirked without saying anything, and Rosebud saw a muscle
above his eye twitch. Forget middle-of-January cold. Her
blood was running Arctic-circle icy.

"Miss Donnelly, at last we meet." Armstrong's smile was
wide—and dangerous, like a shark circling. He looked at
Joe with utter contempt. "I assure you, Miss Donnelly, this
is strictly a business call. I only have business with *you*."

He could bring his muscle, but she couldn't have Joe in the
room? To hell with that. But Rosebud refused to get even one
feather ruffled by this man. "Mr. Thrasher, we have a strict
policy on firearms in the building. Mr. White Thunder will
be happy to escort you to your vehicle, where you can lock
your firearm in your trunk."

Thrasher did that mercenary smirk again, but he held up
his hands in a motion of surrender. "Sure thing." He turned to
Armstrong. "You don't need me here for this part, do you?"

Armstrong gave the wobbly chair a little shake. The chair

wailed in protest, which made Armstrong smile. Rosebud swore she saw a few extra rows of teeth in there. "I think I can manage this just fine."

Manage what? Rosebud would give her left foot to know what the hell this little visit was about. Still, she held her position until Joe and Thrasher were out of the room. "How can I help you today, Mr. Armstrong?"

Still standing, Armstrong opened his briefcase and took out a large manila envelope. "Miss Donnelly, I'm sure you can appreciate that your little legal maneuvers have cost my company a rather large sum of money."

She immediately felt a little better. This territory was more familiar. "Mr. Armstrong, I'm sure you can appreciate that your little dam will cost my entire tribe a place to live."

"That's unfortunate," he said in the same tone of voice one might use to describe three-day-old roadkill. On the one hand, he was creeping her out. On the other hand, she was glad to see her impression of the man had not been wrong. He was a blight upon the land.

He tapped the envelope on the table. "All the same, I'd like to formally ask you, for the last time, to drop all your lawsuits against *my* company."

Rosebud's attention zeroed in on that envelope. If her blood got any colder, it would freeze solid. Where the hell was Dan? "I'm afraid I can't do that, Mr. Armstrong."

Armstrong tilted his head to one side and appraised her. She was not afraid, she repeated to herself.

"Dan mentioned you were a real looker, but I don't think that does you justice."

The clap of fear she felt might as well have been thunder. But she could handle this. She *had* to. "I'm flattered."

Armstrong gave her another dangerous smile. "I have something I want you to see." He slid the envelope over the table.

Instinctively, she knew she didn't want to know what was in there, because whatever it was, it was the end of the world as she knew it. She refused. She wouldn't take it.

Some circuit in her brain must have tripped in the thunderclap, because unexpectedly, she saw her hands reach down and pick up the envelope. *No!* her brain screamed. *Don't open it!*

But her body wasn't listening. Mentally frozen in a state of horror, she saw her hands undo the clasp on the envelope and slide out a short stack of photos.

Of her.

Naked.

With Dan.

A searing pain cut across her forehead, for a second, and all she could think was that she was back in the bar with someone ready to scalp her. Her hand moved up to her forehead and then down to her eyes, but she saw no blood.

"I should think you'd be very flattered," Armstrong was saying. "Some of those are quite good shots. You photograph well. Have you considered a career in modeling?"

The pain got sharper, but her hands kept flipping the pages over and over. Her, stripping off Dan's pants in front of the fire. Her, wiggling out of her jeans. Her, straddling Dan.

Dan, pulling her legs wide apart. Dan, sucking on her nipple. Dan, clearly sliding into her.

"Oh, that's my favorite." Armstrong was still talking, but his voice seemed farther away. "Enough to make me wish I was a younger man. Would have *loved* to have had a run at you in my prime."

She wanted to throw up. She wanted to scream, to fight back, to show this man what a true Lakota woman could do. But she was frozen solid, her body operating mechanically without her express permission.

All she could do was count. Thirteen in all. Thirteen photos of her having sex with Dan.

"There's a jump drive in there, as well." Armstrong's voice seemed to float to her from somewhere in another state. "With the video version on it."

Operating on automatic, her hands tipped the envelope up, and out spilled a small black stick drive. Her, naked, having sex with Dan—screaming. Crying. Being reduced to a babbling idiot, because that's what she'd been—the world's biggest idiot to ever trust a white man. To trust an Armstrong.

And Cecil Armstrong had the pictures to prove just how much of an idiot she'd been. She'd believed Dan when he said he would protect her, when he told her they were safely hidden at the cabin. Lies. All lies. He wasn't even answering her calls now. For all she knew, he was already back in Texas. Maybe he'd already called that Tiffany. Maybe Rosebud had never meant anything to him beyond a means to an end—the end of everything.

"What do you want?" Somehow, she was able to talk.

His voice still seemed far away, but that shark smile was close enough to bite her. "What I want is very simple, Miss Donnelly. I want all past, current and future legal proceedings against Armstrong Holdings dropped. And I'll tell you what else—I'll tell you what I don't want. I don't want to see you in court tomorrow. In fact," he went on, like this whole conversation was the most natural thing in the world, "if you show up, a website named RosebudDonnellyHasSex.com will go live from a remote location. Someone already had the domain name RosebudDoesDan.com," he said with a chuckle.

Scalped alive, that's what this felt like, but instead of taking her hair, he was taking her soul. She'd let herself get conned into falling in love and conned right out of her home, her life.

Her hands were flipping through the photos again, and her

eyes couldn't look away. Dan's face was hard to make out because his head was buried in her breasts in most of the shots, but Armstrong was right. She photographed well. Everybody would see. Everybody would know about her betrayal.

"You've got until tomorrow to think about it. And you can keep those for your scrapbook. I have others." She heard the briefcase shut. "Miss Donnelly, it's been a pleasure." She felt a hand stroke her arm. "A *real* pleasure."

From the other side of the ocean, the door shut. And Rosebud lost the world.

Sixteen

"Maria?" Dan stuck his head into the kitchen. She was where she always was, making something for lunch that promised to be good. A pan of muffins sat cooling next to her, ready to take to Rosebud today. "Cecil's not here. Do you know where he went?"

Maria's head popped up and she looked around like she was worried about something. "No. He left *muy* early today."

"Huh." It was Thursday. If Cecil left the office at all, he did it on Saturday. Something wasn't right. "Thanks," Dan said, digging out his cell phone as he turned to go. He needed to check in with Rosebud.

"Señor Armstrong? I..."

The way Maria said it—all nervouslike—pulled him up short. He turned back around and saw her twisting her hands in her apron. She was always a timid woman, but right now she looked like she was on the verge of disappearing entirely. "What is it?" he asked in his calmest voice.

"I found...*something.*"

The hair on the back of his neck shot to attention. She'd found the *box*. He shut his phone off. "Where is it?" Maria scanned the room again, but no one else was in the house. "Is it here?"

"*Sí*. Come." She led him down into the basement—a place Dan had not been before—and over to a small metal door fastened to the wall. Without speaking, she opened the door and pulled out a garbage bag, which was covered with a thin layer of black dust.

Coal—a coal chute. He'd had no idea it existed. Dan peeled back the bag and there it was. The *box*. Twelve inches wide, three inches deep and almost two feet long, like a safety deposit box from an old, old bank. His pulse picked up the pace. He wasn't sure what was in here, but he had a hunch that it was enough to get Cecil out of the picture and save Rosebud's reservation. "When did you find it?"

"Two days ago." She was still whispering, even though they were in the basement. The whole place reeked of old onions and rotten potatoes.

"And it was here?" Maria might not realize it just yet, but she had the mother of all retention bonuses coming her way. "*How* did you find it?"

At that, she managed to look proud. "It was not in any place I clean. So I started looking in all the places I do not clean."

Dan fought the urge to hug the woman. "The key?" Although the key was secondary. If he had to, he'd bust this damn box open with a sledgehammer—although a busted box was harder to hide from Cecil, if he needed to keep it hidden.

"*Sí*." The basement was dark, but he was sure he saw her wide smile. "Come."

They went back upstairs, Dan clutching the box to his chest. In the sitting room, she stood on tiptoe and reached up behind the mounted buffalo head hanging on the wall. She pulled out a small silver key on an Armstrong Holdings key chain. "I checked. It works."

"Maria, I love you." Which, of course, made her blush like a prairie fire, but he couldn't help it. "You will always have a job with me, okay? But no one knows about this. *No one,* got it?"

"Sí, señor."

Dan all but ran to his room. When he got there, he shoved the old dresser up against the door, just to be safe. Then he sat down on the bed and opened the box.

The first file was filled with detailed schematics for a lakeside resort. Dan stared at the plans in dumb shock. Over four hundred and twenty acres of golf, horseback riding and luxury hotel accommodations—all situated on the edge of the soon-to-be-constructed Dakota Lake. There was even a casino, because part of the resort was located on what was left of the Red Creek reservation.

So that was it. Dan was stunned. He hadn't come close to guessing Cecil's intent, branching out into real estate. The old man was financing construction with Armstrong Holdings money, but the resort would be all his.

He wasn't pushing the dam—he was pushing the reservoir. He was pushing beachfront property in South Dakota.

Finally, Dan set the resort plans aside, confident they would be enough to get Cecil permanently removed from Armstrong Holdings. He picked up the next file. At first, it was just lists of names, some with dates written next to them. He couldn't make heads or tails out of any of it. None of the names rang the slightest of bells. But then the lists began to include dollar figures in the hundreds of thousands next to the dates. The third list had job titles. *Royce Maynard, Chief Judge—$250,000; 4/12/10.*

Holy hell. Cecil had been bribing government officials.

His hands now shaking, Dan kept flipping until he got to a file marked *Indians*. A jump drive fell out when Dan opened the file folder. He grabbed the drive, but didn't get much further into the file before he got to names he recognized.

Rosebud Donnelly. It was circled, with a date written next to it that Dan recognized as his first meeting written above today's date—but no dollar amount. Joe White Thunder was there, as was Emily Mankiller. No money, just circles and dates. Near the back of the file, he found an envelope labeled Tanner Donnelly and dated over three years ago. He opened it and pulled out a set of dog tags.

He closed his eyes, not wanting to see any more. Not that he'd ever doubted Rosebud's murder theory, but there had always been the possibility that his uncle, his family—his *business*—wasn't involved. Not for a dam and not for a resort. But he held the proof in his hands.

Damn his hunches. Always proving themselves right.

There was more—much more—in the box, but Dan made the snap decision that ignorance was not only bliss, but also a matter of self-preservation.

He had to tell someone about this. His first inclination was to call Rosebud, but God only knew what that woman would do with hard evidence. She'd promised not to take another shot at him, but Cecil? Fair game.

He needed the authorities. What had that guy's name been? Tom…Yellow something? Dan dug into his wallet and found the card. Yellow Bird.

He turned his phone back on. One missed call from Rosebud, probably wondering where he was. He glanced at the clock. Man, he was late. Hell, it would take almost as much time to call her as it would to get there, and he needed some serious backup on this issue. Dan dialed Yellow Bird's number and then began putting the files back into the box.

"Yellow Bird," the gruff voice answered.

"This is Armstrong. Dan Armstrong." He locked the box. He couldn't afford to lose any of this, and he couldn't afford to give Cecil the chance to destroy the evidence.

"Officially or unofficially?" Yellow Bird asked after a long pause.

"I found something you've been looking for. I need to get it to the right person." What was that guy's name? Dan raced to his desk and flipped through his files. "Do you know who James Carlson is?"

"Don't jerk my chain, Armstrong." Yellow Bird's voice was sharp, but quieter, like he was trying not to be heard.

Dan bristled. "I can forget the whole damn thing if you'd like, Yellow Bird."

He heard Yellow Bird sniff. "I know Carlson. What do you have?"

"I'm not at liberty to say at this moment." All those weeks with Rosebud were wearing off on him. "Enough," he added.

"I'm going to hold you to that. Give me twenty." The line went dead.

That went well, Dan thought as he shoved his phone in his pocket and wrapped up the box in his pillowcase. If he floored it, he could be at Rosebud's office in twenty. He didn't even stop to grab the muffins.

He held all the winning cards, and he wanted to show her the hand.

The first thing that tipped him off was Judy—more specifically, the fact that she was crying. The second thing was when she looked up and saw him and physically recoiled in horror. The third thing was when she said, "What are you doing here?" like he'd just come back from clubbing baby seals.

If the hair on the back of his neck stood up any more, he'd be halfway to bald. "Is Rosebud here?"

"She left." The hatred in Judy's voice was unmistakable as she scooted back from her desk. If Dan didn't know any better, he'd think the woman was actually afraid of him.

He tried again, hoping to calm her down. "What happened?"

"What happened?" Judy gaped at him like he'd gone stupid. "What *happened* was that you didn't warn us that your uncle and some scary man named Shane Thrasher were going to show up an hour ago. What *happened* was that Joe had to escort that Shane guy out to his car because he had a gun under his coat. What *happened* was that your uncle left five minutes later, smiling like he'd won the freaking lottery, and what *happened* was that ten minutes after that, Rosebud walked out of here like she'd been zombified while you were nowhere to be seen. That's what *happened*."

"My uncle and Thrasher were here?" For a second, he didn't want to believe it. It was just not possible that Cecil would come here—with Thrasher, for God's sake—one day before the court date. The man never got his hands dirty.

"I'm sure you knew all about Cecil's visit, didn't you? Why else weren't you here? Oh, I should have warned Rosebud. I *did.* I told her to be careful with you—but did she listen to me?" Judy was a full five seconds from bolting down the hall, screaming bloody murder. "No. Instead, we let you in here, we let you bring us cookies and brownies, and we let you do…" Here she faltered, but the pause didn't last long enough for Dan to get a word in edgewise. "*Something* to her. And now it's all on *your* head."

She was talking like he'd set up Rosebud. Like he was already guilty just because of his last name. "Judy. You know me. You know I wouldn't do anything to hurt you—any of you." She didn't have a gun, but that hadn't stopped Dan's hands from going up. "Where did she go?"

"I'm not telling you anything. Get out!" Judy picked up the only weapon she had—the coffeepot—and threw it.

He was gone before it smashed behind him.

He'd start with Rosebud's house, he decided as he peeled out of the parking lot. Dan had only been there once—after the bar fight—and everything looked a little different in broad daylight. He tried calling her, but it went straight to voice mail, and he didn't think he could even get close to explaining himself in thirty seconds, so he kept trying.

As the phone rang and rang, he wavered between trying to figure out what Cecil had pulled and not wanting to know. Whatever it was, it was going to be bad. After all, the man had not only bought off public officials, but had even had at least one person killed. If Dan ever saw Thrasher again... Dan checked the glove box. He had enough shotgun shells to do the job right, law be damned.

Finally, he thought he recognized a dirt road. Another half mile down was a house that looked a hell of a lot more like a run-down shack than he remembered. The windows were spider-webbed with tape—more tape than glass, he guessed. No wonder she wouldn't let him visit her. This was what a top-flight lawyer could afford around here?

He was going to make this—all of it—up to her. He had to.

Dan was out the door, hauling the pillow-cased box with him. He was going to need all the backup he could get.

The first thing he noticed was the way a hard silence had come down on the world like a hammer. Nothing made a noise. Not even the wind managed to shush through the weeds.

"Rosebud, please!"

A woman's cry snapped through the silence like a pistol shot. Behind the house. Dan ran around the side just in time to see his Indian princess shake off Emily Mankiller like she was a fly. The older woman landed with a thud on her backside.

Emily saw him, too. During the one awful second when she looked up at him, he saw a world of hurt in her eyes. "No."

It was a warning—but not for Rosebud. For him.

Rosebud froze. She was wearing the buckskin dress with the moccasins. Her hair hung long and loose behind her, the ends blowing in a breeze he couldn't feel. She stood next to her paint horse, the reins in one hand. Her bag was slung over her shoulders.

He couldn't see her other hand.

The whole thing happened in slow motion. She turned around and locked eyes with him. It was like part of her wasn't even there—her eyes were dead. Zombified, Judy had said, and that wasn't far off.

She dropped the reins as her other hand came up, and Dan found himself staring down the barrel of a too-familiar pistol. Instinct kicked in. He let go of the box and stuck his hands up in the air. The box bounced off the tip of his boot, but not hard enough to make him break his stance.

"I should have known better." Her voice was mechanical, and despite how damn quiet the world had gotten, he could barely hear her over the rush of blood in his ears. "I *did* know better, but I…" She blinked at glacial speed, but the pistol didn't waver. "I have no excuse."

"Rosebud, don't!" Emily pleaded again.

"I don't know why you're so surprised. You're the one who told me to get close to him. You're the one who told me to muddle his thinking, to see what I could get out of him. I was just doing what I was told. Like I always do." Rosebud's voice cracked at the end. "I didn't want to. I didn't want to give anything up to you. I thought I could lead you on with a wink and a kiss and not lose who I was. I knew you were trouble, but I couldn't help myself." She laughed, a rote sound that held no pleasure. "I guess that makes me the naive one, doesn't it?"

A small sting quickly blossomed into a gut-clenching pain—not unlike the one time he'd tangled with a scorpion. She had been leading him on—the possibility had never occurred to him. He'd been too caught up in the chase, in the catch, to even realize that she was trying to catch him, too.

"I'm sorry!" Emily's cry was bordering on hysteria. "I didn't want it to be like this!" She turned to Dan. "She never told me anything—nothing about you, I swear!"

The pain dulled, but only a little. He had no idea if he'd been double-crossed. But whether or not Rosebud had set him up was immaterial right now. He might be holding all the cards, but she was the one holding the gun.

He cleared his throat. He might be weaponless but he could still negotiate—although he'd never tried to close a deal when a gun was pointed at him. But he had no choice. "What happened?" Such a simple question. He could only hope it wouldn't get him shot.

Her lips curled up into a feral smile. "How nice of you to ask, but how unnecessary. You've seen the pictures. You helped Cecil set them up. Made sure that Thrasher got a good shot of my face and my…" Her eyes scrunched shut, like she was trying not to see something. He thought he saw her bite her inner lip.

Pictures? Oh, damn. He'd screwed up. He hadn't set her up, but that was immaterial. He'd promised Rosebud he wouldn't let anyone scare her. But he hadn't been able to protect her from his uncle and Thrasher. He'd let her down and, given the drop she had on him, he might not get the chance to apologize, much less make it right.

He made sure to keep his voice level, hoping that some

part of his calm would get through to her. "I didn't set up anything."

"You made me think I could trust you—that you cared about me." She sniffed then. He had no idea if she was crying for herself, or for what she was about to do to him.

"I love you."

"Words," she spat out. The gun jumped an inch, and he fought the urge to take cover. "Lies."

"The truth." She hadn't shot him yet, so he had that going for him. "When the dust settled and we got this dam thing figured out, I was thinking about asking you to marry me." It struck him as funny that it was the truth, but it was.

"You don't want a wife." He could see the tears that were just starting to spill over the edge. "You said so yourself."

"You would never be *just* my wife, darlin'. You will always be my equal."

She softened, and the gun barrel dipped a good half foot. "Dan…"

Keep talking, he prayed. The more she talked, the better chance he stood.

"Whatever he did—whatever pictures he took—I'll make him pay. Believe me, he'll get what's comin' to him."

She trained the gun back on his face. "Fool me once, shame on me. Fool me twice…" She cocked the hammer.

Dan's cell phone rang from deep in his pocket. The unexpected noise made them both jump, and she eased the hammer back down.

"This is important," he said as he slowly dug the phone out of his pocket. She barked out a harsh laugh, but didn't stop him. Yeah, he agreed. What could be more important than being held at gunpoint? But he thought he knew who was calling him. "Armstrong."

"Dan Armstrong?"

"Yeah."

"Carlson here."

"James Carlson?" At the mention of his name, Rosebud jolted with enough force that her horse skittered a step away from her.

"Special counsel for the Department of Justice. Thomas Yellow Bird said you might have something I want."

"Depends on what it is you're looking for."

"Do you know Rosebud Donnelly?"

Dan looked at the woman who was currently not acting in the capacity of a lawyer. "She's here with me now." Rosebud jumped again, the confusion plain on her face. "She contacted you some time ago about her brother's death and a possible connection to my uncle, Cecil Armstrong."

"You sound like a man up-to-date on the situation. Do you have something I can use?"

"Use for what?"

"You tell me what you've got, and I'll let you know if I can use it."

What the hell was this—a game? The arm he was still holding over his head was beginning to tingle. Time to lay his cards on the table. "I found a box of my uncle's. It's got plans for a waterfront resort, as well as lists of names, dates and dollar amounts. I think Tanner Donnelly's dog tags are there, too."

Both women gasped, and Emily broke into tears.

"Dollar amounts?" At least Carlson no longer sounded like he was playing a game of chess.

"I think he bought off some judges to make sure things went his way. I didn't recognize any of the names."

"Mr. Armstrong, you should know that we at the DOJ are pursuing an indictment of Cecil Armstrong and Armstrong Hydro on RICO charges. Your information will be invaluable."

Wait—Armstrong Hydro? It was hard to think straight,

what with the gun and the phone and the sobbing aunt and the zombified Indian princess. "What do I get in return?"

Carlson didn't say anything at first. "What do you want?"

"Leave my company out of this. Cecil left Texas five years ago and has been operating independently ever since."

"I'm not sure I can do that."

"Then I burn the box."

"That's uncalled for, Mr. Armstrong."

His hand was completely asleep now, but Rosebud still had the gun trained on him. "I'll give you all the evidence I have if you leave my company out of it. And you have to leave Rosebud out of it, too."

Another pause, this time longer. Dan wondered if the call was being recorded or traced. "Now why would I *have* to do that?"

"I think Cecil's trying to blackmail her." She jabbed the gun in his direction again, but this time he saw past it. Her face—blotchy and red and furious and hurt—told him he was spot-on. "I think he's got photos of her—compromising photos. I want them destroyed. No one else sees them. No one."

"Who else is in them?"

Dan swallowed the last shred of his pride. "Me."

Carlson said nothing for a painful minute. "You said she's there?"

"Yes."

"What's she doing?"

"Well, right now, she's got a gun pointed at me."

Carlson whistled. "Those must be some photos. Let me talk to her."

"James Carlson wants to talk to you," Dan told Rosebud. Moving as slowly as he could, he held out the phone.

Maybe her hand was getting tired, too, because the gun

was anything but steady. In one quick motion, she reached out and snatched the phone from him. "It's me."

Me? Something about the way she said it hit Dan as more than just two lawyers talking, but he was in no position to get his nose bent out of shape about it.

"No, I—yes." She scrunched her eyes shut tight, and for some reason, Dan was reminded of the first time he'd recognized her in the parking lot. She looked miserable, but her voice didn't waver at all—just like when she'd lost it after the bar fight and told him she hoped crying didn't affect his opinion of her in the courtroom. "They're awful, James. Everything. *Everything.*"

Thrasher must have found the cabin. That was the only logical explanation. He must have found the cabin, and them in it.

One box of shotgun shells wasn't going to be enough.

"He said—" Here she hiccupped, but had herself back under control in a second. "Cecil said that if I showed up in court tomorrow, he had a website that was going to go live. He has…he has video." She managed to get the last bit out, but finally the sobs had started.

Hot rage filled him. It was one thing to have pictures of him—but what Cecil was doing to Rosebud was beyond the pale. He had to pay—him and Thrasher.

"But I—yeah. Yeah. Do I have your word?" In no great hurry, she lowered her weapon. "I know. I understand. I will. No, I won't. Promise." Gun finally pointing at the ground, she held the phone out to him. "He wants to talk to you again."

Dan's first instinct was to get the gun, but sudden movement seemed like a bad idea right now, considering the fingers on one hand had completely fallen asleep. "Carlson?"

"Here's the deal, Armstrong. You give me Cecil, and you can keep your company. The company will plead no contest to bribing public officials and will be fined for an amount equal to, but not greater than, the amount of money paid in bribes."

"And Rosebud?"

"I can't destroy the photos—yet. I explained to her that blackmail is a serious charge. But I'll hold them under lock and key, and I promise they will never be made public."

"How do I know I can trust you?"

"Didn't she tell you about me?"

The lightbulb went off. "James—from law school?"

Rosebud nodded.

"I promise you—I won't let this out. But we need the site to go live, at least for a few minutes. She's got to go to court tomorrow."

"No."

"Five minutes, that's all I'm asking. Five minutes, and we'll have enough to put him away on blackmail alone. She's already agreed."

"Is that what you want?" he asked Rosebud.

"I made a mistake," she said. Her voice was as flat as three-day-old soda. "This is the price I've got to pay."

"Oh, and I told her not to shoot you," Carlson added as an afterthought. "You're a material witness now."

"Thanks. What about Cecil?"

"Yellow Bird is on his way to get the evidence. The moment the site goes live, we'll arrest Cecil. Yellow Bird thinks a man named Thrasher is our hit man, so we'll pick him up then, too."

Damn it. He wouldn't get the chance to make Thrasher beg for his life. He could only hope Yellow Bird would do it for him. "What do you want me to do?"

"Humor the old man—and don't kill him, okay? This is bigger than just your uncle. Yellow Bird has the details."

Chief Judge, that one entry had said. "You're going to roll him?"

Carlson exhaled into the phone, a man tired by a long fight. "I'm going to try. Either way, I need him alive. Can you do that, or do I need to send Yellow Bird to pick you up, too?"

Not killing Cecil was asking a lot of a man, but Rosebud was staring at him. "I get the company, Rosebud stays out of it and you get Cecil. That's the deal?"

"That's the deal."

"Done."

"I'll be in touch."

"What happened?" Emily had managed to right herself. She edged toward Rosebud. "Dear?"

"I…" Rosebud looked down at her hand and seemed to notice she was holding a gun. "Oh. I'm—I said I wouldn't do that again."

Considering the circumstances, he wasn't sure if an incoherent Rosebud was such a good thing or not. "It's all right."

"It's not! I— Oh, my God. I messed up. I messed up everything." Unexpectedly, she whirled, leaping onto her paint's back with surprising agility, considering the horse wasn't even wearing a saddle. The horse reared back, just enough that Dan could see she still had the gun in her hand. Then the two of them took off down the road before cutting through some tall grass and disappearing behind a low hill.

Something clamped down on his arm. It was only then that he realized he'd tried to run after her. He looked down to see Emily's strong hand gripping him. "No," she said again. "It's not safe for you."

"Not safe for me?" As if the last ten minutes had been a picnic? He shook her off—but not so hard that she lost her footing. "You tried to set me up."

Her eyes went wide in alarm. "We didn't know—"

His phone rang. Giving Emily a final glare, he walked away and did the only thing he could.

He answered it.

Seventeen

Cecil's yahoo lawyer said something and the old man laughed. It took every last bit of Dan's self-control not to crack those two heads together, and he was running low in the self-control department right now. He was operating on less than two hours of broken sleep. Every time his eyes had closed last night, he'd seen Rosebud's face, flitting between dangerously blank and shattered. He'd started awake, and then lain there, wondering where she was and if she was okay. She wasn't answering her phone, and he'd stopped checking with Emily at midnight.

He was having a hard time figuring out where to look in the courtroom. If he looked straight ahead, he'd be staring at Cecil, and he couldn't look at Cecil without the world getting red around the edges. He was real proud of the fact that, when Cecil had asked him yesterday evening how his meeting with "that Donnelly woman" had gone with a sick smile on his face, Dan had come up with some load of bull about her not feeling well. Thomas Yellow Bird had said to be clueless, so Dan was doing clueless. So far, Cecil was buying it.

If Dan looked to his left, he'd be forced to look at Thrasher, making a whole hell of a lot more than just the edges of the world go red. Dan wanted to reach across the divider and rip that slime-filled smile right off his face. Slowly.

If Dan looked to his right, he'd see the spot where Rosebud was supposed to be preparing for her court case today. The table was empty. No one from the tribe was here. Not even Councilwoman Emily Mankiller.

He'd desperately wanted to go after Rosebud, but Yellow Bird had called. Dan had to hand over the box and be convinced not to go all vigilante on the assholes sitting less than two feet in front of him. He wasn't supposed to alarm Cecil, so he'd been forced to have dinner with the man, forced to fake mild confusion at Rosebud's sudden "illness" right before the big day and forced not to sneak out and go looking for her. Hell, it had been hard enough answering his cell phone without spooking Cecil.

Cecil and Thrasher would be taken care of by the justice system. His company was in the clear and the tribe would keep their land. This was supposed to be the big victory. It didn't feel like it, though. Not yet. How was he supposed to fix the mess still between him and Rosebud when he couldn't even find out where she'd gone? He got that she was upset. Hell, he was furious about the whole thing. She'd taken a big risk by trusting him, and it had blown up on her. But she *had* to know it wasn't his fault. He had to prove to her that he was the man she'd fallen in love with, the man she could still trust.

He wanted them to leave here, get away from the memories they were both desperate to forget and make some new ones, untainted ones. They could go back to his estate in Texas. He'd introduce her to his mother, and Rosebud would see then that Dan wasn't an Armstrong like Cecil, but one like his father and his mother, someone better. Someone who would honor her as long as they both lived.

But he couldn't apologize, much less propose, if he couldn't find her.

Aside from a few local reporters, Yellow Bird was the only other person in the courtroom. He was sprawled out on a bench three rows behind Dan. Yellow Bird had found the one spot in the courtroom that streamed sunlight, so he had on his shades. Dan couldn't tell if Yellow Bird was watching him or Cecil, but he was pretty sure Yellow Bird had orders to shoot either of them if the setup went south.

"All rise," the bailiff intoned. "The Honorable Royce Maynard, presiding."

Dan did a double-take as he stood. Royce Maynard? Damn it all. Dan should have immediately realized that the judge on Cecil's list was the one presiding over the trial today. That meant that Rosebud would have lost her case today, no matter what. They wouldn't have been able to stop Cecil if Maria hadn't found the lockbox of evidence.

Dan had no idea what to think about Rosebud's disappearance. On the one hand, if Rosebud made it, the site would go live. He didn't want her to have to go through that, but he wanted to see her again. He needed one more chance to convince her that he'd do anything for her.

On the other, if she didn't show, they'd lose the blackmail charge, what Carlson had called the kind of insurance money couldn't buy. There was a small chance Cecil would go free without the blackmail charge as backup. If that happened, Dan would have a very hard time stopping the construction that was ready to begin. But at least Rosebud's public humiliation level would be a hell of a lot lower.

"Court is now in session," the bailiff said as Judge Maynard settled his considerable girth onto the bench.

"Be seated." Maynard glared at the lopsided courtroom. "Where is the attorney for the Red Creek tribe?"

Dan kept his face as benign as possible. On the take, but putting on a hell of a show. This country didn't need crooks ruling on matters of life and death, because that's what this was. A matter of life and death for her tribe. If she didn't show up…

"Here," a thin voice called out from the back of the courtroom. "I'm here, Your Honor."

Dan spun in his seat. Rosebud stood in the doorway, wearing her one-and-only suit. She had a white-knuckle grip on her briefcase, but her face was unreadable, betraying no emotion of any kind. She had her game face on, that much was clear as she walked into the room with the same confidence he'd been confronted with when he'd first accused her of shooting his hat. She could do this, he realized. Pride swelled in his chest as he watched her walk down the aisle.

She was the most amazing woman he'd ever met.

As she passed him, however, he got a better look at her. Her confidence didn't reach her eyes. In fact, her eyes didn't move. They didn't see him, Cecil or even the judge. Dan wasn't sure she was even *in* there. It might not be obvious to anyone except him, but she was operating on autopilot.

He saw blood red again as his gaze swung back to Cecil. At least he didn't have a gun—and he was sure Rosebud didn't, either. She couldn't have gotten one past the metal detector—he hoped.

Cecil snorted as Rosebud sat down at her table. He leaned over and whispered something to Thrasher that made him laugh out loud before Cecil pulled out his cell phone and made the all-important call.

"You're late, Ms. Donnelly." Judge Maynard's voice boomed into the room.

"My apologies to the court," Rosebud said. Her voice was

strong and confident. Despite it all, she was still one hell of a lawyer.

"Mr. Armstrong, court is in session," Maynard boomed even louder. "Whatever it is, it can wait."

"Of course, Your Honor." Cecil snapped his phone shut and sat there looking smug.

Dan wasn't going to make it without punching someone. That phone call was obviously related to the site going live, just like Cecil had promised. Everything was going according to plan, but Dan wasn't sure how much more of this plan he could take. He wanted Rosebud back. He wanted to show her that he hadn't set her up. He wanted Cecil and Thrasher to pay.

He wanted blood.

The judge asked if either side had a statement. To Dan's surprise, Rosebud said, "Yes." She stood. "Your Honor, the Lakota have survived smallpox, the iron horse and the United States Army. We survived the Black Hills gold rush, the death of the buffalo and the reservation. We have survived the white man's schools, his treaties and his greed."

She was doing it, he marveled, defending her case while Cecil ground her dignity into the dust. Whatever happened between them after this was over, he'd do his damndest to make sure she knew how proud he was of her.

"We have survived…" Her eyes scrunched shut, but her voice remained strong. "Intimidation, murder and blackmail."

Someone snorted. Dan thought it was Thrasher. Rosebud didn't appear to hear it. "We, the people of the Red Creek Lakota, have endured in the face of tragedy and horror. But if you allow the Dakota River to be dammed and the land flooded, you will sentence us to a fate worse than personal…" she paused long enough to clear her throat "…embarrassment, a fate worse than death. You will be accomplishing what all white men before you have failed to do—you will be condemning us to oblivion. You will erase the Red Creek tribe."

A swell of pride surged up in Dan's chest and managed to block out his simmering rage. Cecil hadn't beaten her. How could he have ever thought the old man could? She was stronger than that. He ached in ways he hadn't thought possible. She had to know he loved her, right?

The lawyer representing Dan's company got up and began to talk in bold, sweeping terms about "progress" and "action." Dan sat, not moving a muscle, because if he moved, he would lunge, and if he lunged, Yellow Bird would probably shoot him in the butt.

The lawyer droned on and on. All the while, Dan wondered what the hell Carlson was waiting for. Where was he? The website had to have gone live by now—what else did he need?

"I've reviewed the case," Maynard said after the yahoo lawyer finally sat down. "I find that the grounds for a preliminary injunction against Armstrong Hydro are baseless. Judgment for the defendant."

Time seemed to slow down as the gavel swung. Dan had just enough time to think, *this is it,* before the courtroom doors slammed open behind him. Suddenly, the number of people in the courtroom jumped as uniformed officers rushed in.

About time, Dan thought, as he shot out of his seat. He had to get to Rosebud. Now.

"What is going on here? Order! *Order!*" Maynard howled as he banged the gavel.

Dan jumped the barrier, dodging an officer and hoping he wasn't about to get shot. "Rosebud," he said as he knelt before her.

Her eyes closed as her head tilted away from him. Nope—she wasn't going to pull that stoic crap on him, not after everything they'd been through. He hadn't done anything wrong, damn it. He *loved* her.

"*Look* at me," he ordered. He managed to keep his voice gentle, but only just.

A tall man wearing an expensive suit strode into the room. "Your Honor, James Carlson, special counsel for the Department of Justice. I have a warrant of arrest for Cecil Armstrong." He handed the warrant to Cecil, who dropped it like it was radioactive.

"A warrant? On what charges?" Wasn't that just like Cecil, Dan thought. Ballsy to the very end.

Suddenly, shouts of "Get down, get down!" filled the room. A shot rang out. Without thinking, Dan threw his body over Rosebud's, knocking her off her chair and onto the floor. She grunted as he landed on top of her.

"Are you okay?" he asked, even as he realized it was a dumb question. So he tried again, searching her face. "Are you hurt?"

Her body was stiff under his, and her eyes scrunched shut tight. Maybe her confidence had been more bravado than he'd thought, because she looked like she was about to pass out. Then she said, "Just…tell me when it's over."

The pain that racked her voice cut through all Dan's redness, through the shouting and the sound of furniture scraping and breaking. At that moment, nothing in the world mattered as much as Rosebud. Screw everything—Cecil, the company, the dam—all of it. The only thing he cared about was this woman. His woman.

"I will. I won't let them hurt you anymore."

Nodding, she swallowed—and turned her face into Dan's neck. Her whole body curled into his, and suddenly she was right back where she belonged.

For what felt like the first time today, he took a deep breath. "It's okay," he murmured as he wrapped his arms around her. She clutched his jacket, pulling him closer. Relief flooded his system. "I'm here. You're here. You were amazing. Ferocious in the courtroom."

"I had to," she whispered, her breath warm against his skin. "I had to do it for the tribe. For Tanner." A piece of wood snapped and someone groaned. She shuddered. "Don't leave me."

She still needed him. She still trusted him. He pulled her as far into his arms as he could without crushing her. He didn't know if the gunfire was over or not, but he'd take whatever came his way—anything to keep her safe. "I won't."

Shouting was followed by the splintering of more wood giving up the fight, and then there was a moment of awkward calm. Dan hazarded a look over his shoulder.

Yellow Bird had Thrasher on the ground, a knee against his neck. One of them was bleeding, but no one acted like it was fatal. "I've been waiting three years to say this, you dog. You're under arrest for the murder of Tanner Donnelly," Yellow Bird said through gritted teeth.

Rosebud's chest heaved against his. "Is it over yet?"

"Almost, babe. Almost." For her sake, he prayed it was true.

"Bailiff, holster your weapon and clear this courtroom!" Maynard roared. "Now!"

Carlson stepped up to the bench and handed Maynard his own piece of paper. "Your Honor, with all due respect, he can't do that. You're under arrest for accepting bribes."

"Get your hands off me!" It was wrong to find so much satisfaction in the note of terror in Cecil's voice. But Dan found it anyway. "Dan, do something!"

"I'm not going anywhere," Dan whispered. He gave Rosebud a final squeeze before he rose and pivoted on the balls of his feet. Keeping one hand on her arm, he made sure his body was between her and his uncle. She remained curled against his back as he surveyed the room. The place was in shambles—more like a raid in a drug den than a house of law.

"Dan." Cecil still sounded defiant.

Dan glanced at his uncle. Cecil's arms were cuffed behind him. Yellow Bird was just hauling Thrasher to his feet. The bailiff, who had a bloody nose, had his gun trained on that slime-bag. Thrasher must have tried to get the bailiff's weapon. Even Maynard had his hands up, the sleeves of his robe pooling in his armpits as an officer read him his rights.

"Dan?" Cecil said again. The defiance was fading fast, replaced with stark terror. "Dan, please—I'm your uncle! We're kin!"

Go on, Dan thought. *I want you to beg.* But he didn't say it, because that wasn't what Rosebud needed to hear. He turned his attention back to her. "It's safe now," he said, keeping his voice as calm as he could. "He can't hurt you anymore."

A stream of curse words burst out of the old man's chest, but Dan didn't pay him any mind. He waited for Rosebud.

It was her move.

Even though Rosebud was behind Dan, he kept his hands on her arms, making sure she was protected. She didn't want to look. She didn't want to see if someone had been killed, didn't want to see Cecil Armstrong or Shane Thrasher. She didn't want to see any guns, and she didn't want to see if one was pointed at her or Dan.

For a fleeting, incomprehensible second, she had a powerful urge to click her heels together and say, "There's no place like home," as if that would magically make this whole awful week disappear into thin air.

"Ms. Donnelly?" James asked, sounding very much like the lawyer he was now, not the lover he'd once been. "Are you unhurt?"

Right. James was here. Dan was here. Cecil was here, for

God's sake—unless someone had shot him. No amount of
ruby-red slippers would whisk her away from this, so she'd
better snap out of it. She let herself breathe in Dan's scent
before she pushed herself away from his back. His hands
dropped to his sides.

"Mr. Carlson," she said.

On one hand, the formality was ridiculous. James had seen
her naked, after all, and had probably looked at those photos
to boot. On the other hand, the only other person in the world
who knew that James had seen her naked was Dan. As far
as the rest of the world was concerned, James Carlson and
Rosebud Donnelly had gone to law school together—nothing more than that—and she was damn sure going to keep it
that way.

She took a second to straighten her skirt and dust off her
jacket before she stepped around Dan. That one second gave
her a chance to compose herself and put on her game face,
something that now felt foreign and stiff. She didn't feel like
the lawyer she used to be. She didn't want to be a ball-buster
anymore. Her life wasn't her case—the case was over, but
she was still standing. Problem was, she didn't know what
else she could do.

Well, first things first, and the first thing was to get the
hell out of this courtroom. She squared her shoulders and
stuck out her chin as she opened her eyes. The extent of the
damage immediately made her wish she hadn't. The courtroom looked like downtown Baghdad. The barrier was crum-
pled against the first row of spectator seats. The defendant's
table was in about forty pieces. And, of course, there were a
few deputies aiming guns with the safeties off.

In the middle stood James. He looked older, his hair already picking up some salt at the temples. He seemed more
like a politician now, and with this sort of coup, he'd be in a
position to run for office. He'd be good at that, she thought.

He smiled at her—not that anyone else could tell, but she knew that when his lips thinned like that, he was pleased. And looking around at three years of his hard work in handcuffs, Rosebud knew he was very pleased.

"Ms. Donnelly, your government thanks you for your patience in this matter," he said, extending his hand for a formal handshake. "I want to personally thank you for your cooperation."

"I expect justice to be served," she said, feeling the barest hint of warmth spread from his hand to hers. He'd never loved her, that she knew. But he'd cared for her. And as he patted the top of her hand, she knew that he still cared for her. "I held up my end of the deal. May I safely assume you held up yours?"

He gave her hand a squeeze, which had the same effect as a comforting hug. "The site was live for one minute before I took it down personally," he replied. "No one saw."

Rosebud felt herself breathe for the first time in what felt like days. "I expect it to stay that way."

"Absolutely." He glanced toward Dan, the look on his face somewhere between jealous and all business as he gave her hand one last squeeze.

Rosebud got the hint. She turned to Dan and held out her hand. Without hesitation, he laced his fingers with hers and stepped up until he was standing hip-to-hip with her. Immediately, she felt his warmth surround her. She felt safe with him beside her—like nothing bad could happen. He rubbed his thumb over her knuckles as she said, "Have you met Dan Armstrong?"

"Not in person. Mr. Armstrong," James said as the two men shook hands. "The Department of Justice owes you a debt of gratitude for everything you've done here."

Rosebud couldn't help but notice that the grip went on a little too long—and that both men were clenching their jaws.

Men, she thought with an inner snort of disgust. Even so, she felt a little flattered, in a primeval sort of way.

A strange noise drew her attention away from Dan and James. It sounded like someone was strangling a cat.

"You did this?" Ah. Cecil Armstrong was all but blue in the face as he sputtered. *"You?"*

In a flash, Rosebud didn't so much *see* as *feel* the victory. After three long years, justice was served. A sense of righteous power flowed through her. She'd won. All it had cost her was…everything. Her brother, her life for all those years, her dignity…

The righteousness was short-lived. So she'd won.

Now what?

Then Dan settled his hand around her waist and pulled her in close. "We had a deal, Carlson."

"So we did." James's eyes cut from Dan back to Rosebud. "You have my word."

Dan shook his hand again as Cecil went from bluish to a bruised purple. Not that Dan noticed. He was focused on James. "Do you need either of us for anything else?"

"I think we're good. We've got the box."

"You!" Cecil was stuck on the one word, apparently. Good, Rosebud thought. He could just be stuck—for the rest of his life. He went well past conniption fit and into hysterics.

Dan had been working *with* James. He'd been working *against* Cecil. Somehow, in the midst of her embarrassment and turmoil, she'd gotten things wrong. Dan hadn't set her up—far from it. He'd been with her the whole time. He'd stuck to the plan, just like he'd said he would. After all, he was a man of his word. The back of her neck flushed hot.

"Where can I reach you?" James asked, also ignoring the impotent old man in shackles. Because that's what Cecil was now. Dan was right. Cecil Armstrong couldn't hurt her anymore, not as long as Dan was by her side.

Dan let go of her waist long enough to fish out his card. Two, actually. "That's my cell, and the other one is Betty Armstrong's home number. She's my mother. You can reach me and Rosebud there."

"Wait, what?" His mother was in Texas. Suddenly, Rosebud didn't know what was happening again.

Dan looked down at her and grinned. His hand wrapped around hers. Rosebud felt the flush spread all the way down her back. "I promised her I wouldn't marry you before she met you, so I thought we'd better get that out of the way, real quicklike." He turned his attention back to James. "We can go to Texas, right?"

Dan was going take her to meet his mother. He was going to marry her—real quicklike. "If you want to go to Texas," he added, his voice dropping several notches as his fingers tightened around her hand. "Do you want to go with me?"

James regarded them both with a stern eye. "Ms. Donnelly, we will not be pressing charges against Dan Armstrong. We believe he had no knowledge in *any* of Cecil Armstrong's illicit activities."

Somewhere in the next world, Tanner was nodding with approval.

Dan hadn't known about the photos. Dan had nothing to do with that awful website. Dan, she knew now, deep in her soul, hadn't set her up.

Dan wanted to marry her.

James cleared his throat. "Ms. Donnelly, do you want to go to Texas with Mr. Armstrong?" Nothing like a little cross-examination during the most important moment of her life.

Everyone in what remained of the courtroom stood silent. Even Cecil Armstrong was quiet, his mouth wordlessly opening and shutting as the world waited on her answer.

"Come with me," Dan whispered. "Just you and me. Dan and Rosebud. That's all I want. That's all I've ever wanted."

She opened her mouth, but nothing came out.

She closed her eyes and breathed. Sandalwood and musk—Dan's scent—filled her nose. Her hand found his chest and she felt his heart pounding. She knew if she leaned forward just a little, she'd be able to taste his breath with a kiss.

She leaned against Dan's chest, letting a flush steal over her body.

Just Dan and Rosebud.

Right now, that was all she wanted, too.

"Mr. Carlson, if you need me, I'll be in Texas."

Epilogue

In December, Shane Thrasher pled guilty to first-degree manslaughter, among other charges, and was sentenced to twenty-five years in jail, with the possibility of parole. In exchange for his plea, he testified about the work he'd done for Cecil Armstrong for four years. He was on the stand for six days.

Almost a year later, Cecil Armstrong was convicted of racketeering, bribing officials and conspiracy to commit murder, among other charges. He was sentenced to thirty-five years in prison without the possibility of parole, which, given the fact that he was seventy-three at the time, amounted to a life sentence. An audit of his books had revealed he'd misappropriated millions of Armstrong Holdings' funds in his pursuit of beachfront property in the middle of South Dakota. However, he never offered up any justification for his actions.

The only member of the Armstrong family in court that day was Betty Armstrong. She held hands with Emily

Mankiller as the sentence was handed down. Both women were escorted from the courtroom by Thomas Yellow Bird and offered no comment to the throngs of reporters waiting outside.

The sensationalist nationwide coverage of the trial led to a measurable uptick of visitors to the Historic Bonneau Homestead and Museum, former headquarters of Armstrong Hydro. The museum's curator and caretaker, Maria Villerreal, reported that, on average, a hundred visitors a day were coming to listen to her tours. Her sons made pocket money selling homemade cookies and lemonade. On the day her former boss was sentenced, no fewer than thirty reporters crowded the house. Maria gave them all brownies, but not a comment on the trial or her current employers.

Dan Armstrong was too busy to attend the trial, except on days when he was called to testify. He divided his time between Armstrong Petroleum in Witchita Falls, Texas, and Armstrong Hydro in Sioux Falls, South Dakota. At the time of the sentencing, he was busy supervising construction of the Red Creek dam, a run-of-river dam on the Dakota ten miles south of the Red Creek Indian reservation. The Red Creek tribe owned half the dam, and more than half of the workers were members of the tribe. Joe White Thunder was out there with them, swinging a hammer in time like he was beating a drum.

Rosebud Armstrong chose to avoid the lengthy trial entirely. Instead, she focused her efforts on joining an ongoing multitribal lawsuit against the Bureau of Indian Affairs for mismanagement of tribal funds. The case had already made it through the U.S. Court of Appeals on its way to the Supreme Court, where Rosebud became the first woman from her tribe to argue—and win—a case before the High Court. She discovered a renewed passion for the law, now that her life no longer depended on the outcome. She began to enjoy herself again.

After that sweeping victory, she took some doctor-ordered time off. On the day they led Cecil away in shackles, she sat in the nursery of the new ranch house that overlooked the Dakota River and finished Tanner's baby quilt. Lewis's was already on the crib. The twins were due in two weeks, but given how much they kicked, she hadn't been sure she'd make it. At first, the bed rest had driven her nuts. But she'd taken up her needle and thread again, rediscovering a part of her that she'd thought she'd lost.

She was happy here in this new home built on neutral territory, just Dan and Rosebud. Her family was close by, and they made frequent trips to Texas. It had become all she'd ever wanted.

Soon enough, though, it would be Dan and Rosebud and Tanner and Lewis.

She was more than happy here.

She was home.

* * * * *

PASSION

For a spicier, decidedly hotter read—
this is your destination for romance!

COMING NEXT MONTH
AVAILABLE JANUARY 10, 2012

#2131 TERMS OF ENGAGEMENT
Ann Major

#2132 SEX, LIES AND THE SOUTHERN BELLE
Dynasties: The Kincaids
Kathie DeNosky

#2133 THE NANNY BOMBSHELL
Billionaires and Babies
Michelle Celmer

#2134 A COWBOY COMES HOME
Colorado Cattle Barons
Barbara Dunlop

#2135 INTO HIS PRIVATE DOMAIN
The Men of Wolff Mountain
Janice Maynard

#2136 A SECRET BIRTHRIGHT
Olivia Gates

You can find more information on upcoming Harlequin® titles,
free excerpts and more at www.HarlequinInsideRomance.com.

HDCNM1211

Brittany Grayson survived a horrible ordeal at the hands of a serial killer known as The Professional... who's after her now?

Harlequin® Romantic Suspense presents a new installment in Carla Cassidy's reader-favorite miniseries,
LAWMEN OF BLACK ROCK.

Enjoy a sneak peek of
TOOL BELT DEFENDER.

Available January 2012
from Harlequin® Romantic Suspense.

"**B**rittany?" His voice was deep and pleasant and made her realize she'd been staring at him openmouthed through the screen door.

"Yes, I'm Brittany and you must be…" Her mind suddenly went blank.

"Alex. Alex Crawford, Chad's friend. You called him about a deck?"

As she unlocked the screen, she realized she wasn't quite ready yet to allow a stranger inside, especially a male stranger.

"Yes, I did. It's nice to meet you, Alex. Let's walk around back and I'll show you what I have in mind," she said. She frowned as she realized there was no car in her driveway. "Did you walk here?" she asked.

His eyes were a warm blue that stood out against his tanned face and was complemented by his slightly shaggy dark hair. "I live three doors up." He pointed up the street to the Walker home that had been on the market for a while.

"How long have you lived there?"

"I moved in about six weeks ago," he replied as they

walked around the side of the house.

That explained why she didn't know the Walkers had moved out and Mr. Hard Body had moved in. Six weeks ago she'd still been living at her brother Benjamin's house trying to heal from the trauma she'd lived through.

As they reached the backyard she motioned toward the broken brick patio just outside the back door. "What I'd like is a wooden deck big enough to hold a barbecue pit and an umbrella table and, of course, lots of people."

He nodded and pulled a tape measure from his tool belt. "An outdoor entertainment area," he said.

"Exactly," she replied and watched as he began to walk the site. The last thing Brittany had wanted to think about over the past eight months of her life was men. But looking at Alex Crawford definitely gave her a slight flutter of pure feminine pleasure.

Will Brittany be able to heal in the arms of Alex,
her hotter-than-sin handyman...or will a second
psychopath silence her forever? Find out in
TOOL BELT DEFENDER
Available January 2012
from Harlequin® Romantic Suspense
wherever books are sold.